John S. Rae

Poems and Songs

John S. Rae

Poems and Songs

ISBN/EAN: 9783744766593

Printed in Europe, USA, Canada, Australia, Japan

Cover: Foto ©Andreas Hilbeck / pixelio.de

More available books at **www.hansebooks.com**

POEMS AND SONGS

BY

JOHN S. RAE.

WITH INTRODUCTION BY

D. H. EDWARDS, F.R.H.S., &c.,

Editor of " Modern Scottish Poets "

BRECHIN :
PRINTED AT THE ADVERTISER OFFICE.
EDINBURGH : JOHN MENZIES & CO.
1884.

PREFACE.

—◇—

N laying this selection of my Poems and Songs before my fellowmen, I have not been actuated by the vainglory of mere authorship, nor the desire of gain. Were these the only motives that prompted writers to bring their musings to the light, they might naturally be expected to be of such a nature as would fit them more to feast the moth than feed the minds of men. The pleasure I have found in "courting the Muses," began to shed its charms around my path when about midway in my teens ; and whether in the peaceful seclusion of the country, or amid the smoke-dimmed haunts of busy cities, vocal with the thousand-tongued voice of commerce, that pleasure has been my soothing companion at all times ; and if these fruits of my lonely leisure hours, embodied in song,

> . . . Can cheer one heart
> That listens to my strain,
> I cherish will the sweet belief
> I have not sung in vain.

Mine have not been days of rural quiet, spent in sylvan nooks "far from the madding crowd's ignoble strife," still the Muse deigned to find me and cheer me amid "the busy haunts of men ;" and although what she breathed may not be faultless, I, as her interpreter, must bear the blame, being through lack of leisure at times compelled to hastily clothe these children of my mind lest they should perish of neglect. These Poems and Songs have therefore the merit at least of being the spontaneous effusions of a son of "Caledonia stern and wild," whose love for her rugged hills and spreading moorlands, for her name and fame, her history and traditions, shall only cease with his own existence.

JOHN S. RAE.

BURNGRAINS, ALVAH,
BANFF, *November*, 1884.

CONTENTS.

INTRODUCTION.

—◇—

" A drainless shower
Of light is poesy ; 'tis the supreme of power ;
'Tis might half slumbering on its own right arm."

IN these lines Keats expresses his belief that poesy is the regal faculty of human nature—a faculty so powerful that it can afford to "slumber on its own right arm." Men have been criticising and defining poetry for more than two thousand years, yet to-day it is by no means a settled point that its radical characteristics are this or that. To define it anew is not at this time our object, nor do we presume to be a champion of any critical school. Poetry, by its nature, holds by faith, and works by love. Whether as feeling in the human breast, or as the music that ravishes or overcomes, poetry does not deal with proof, but with acceptation. Poetry is the daughter of imagination—not of the faculty that reasons and discovers, but of that which sees and frames. It is the caroling and leaping of the child when the heart is full of joy ; the dirge of the hero, chanted to sky and ocean when the grief that lies on his soul can roll off only in waves as of a swelling sea. The feeling scorns bounds and measurements. The expression leaves the common prose-road, enters the sun-chariot, and rhythmically rolls along. The god of Poetry did not tread on the plain ground. Apollo rode through the azure in his car of fire. According to Lamartine, " Poetry is man himself, the instinct of all his epochs, the eternal echo of all his human impressions, the voice of thinking and feeling humanity, resumed and modulated by certain men."

Poetry is not a quantum of intelligible propositions; it is not to be apprehended through the logical understanding, but through the feelings. To him who does not feel a poem for himself it is hopeless to explain its meaning; the most intelligent may be as dull to poetry as Dr Johnson was to Milton's sonnets, of which he wrote that "the only thing to be said about the best was that they were not bad." Yet, though poetry, as Mark Pattison says, "is to be apprehended by the feelings, it does not follow that every one is born with or without the feelings that can enjoy poetry, and that a reader of poetry, like a poet, is born, not made." The first qualification for the reading of a book of poetry is a quick and ready sympathy for actualities. What the poet, in fact, does for us is to express with greater vividness, keenness, and passion our experiences. We admire him because he has a wide horizon of vision, and a more intense capacity of being moved by the same objects which, in a less degree, move ourselves.

What is colouring without eyes, melody without ears, or fragrance without the living sense to appreciate? The glories of the world without, whether of art or of Nature, are but the glories of the world within, kindled and reflected, and made alive in the sentient, imaginative soul. A happy, lively, and warmly susceptible spirit, in contact with the beauties, and odours, and harmonies of Nature, cannot but feel that it is ever melodious, and welling over with freshness, lightness, and emotional joy.

George Sand, the celebrated French author, says : "They tell us that Poetry is dying—but Poetry cannot die. Had she for place of sojourn one human heart, there would still be ages of existence before her ; for she would issue thence like the lava of a volcano, and strike out a path to herself. . . . . . . Weary of uttering a language which the great no longer comprehend, she will murmur, in the ears of the humble, words of affection and sympathy." And has not this been so in Scotland in modern times? In many cases Poetry has taken refuge with the humble. She has cradled in her arms the children of the poor, and intermingled herself with the simple details of their daily life. It is, indeed, one of the most pleasing characteristics of our present-day national poets that they aim at interpreting in verse the common interests of the common day, and the equally common, but withal eternal, instincts of the human heart in those endless manifestations which make up the many-threaded web of life. And is it not the case that the man of sympathetic feeling does more to fulfil " man's chief end " than he who, amidst the smoke of battle, earns a wreath to deck his crown? Ever since the human soul was first cap¸ able of feeling the alternate impulse of pain and pleasure, happiness and sorrow, or hope and despair, a poetical effusion naturally gives it relief. All whose hearts are in the right place—who can realise that "under the snow-drifts the flowers are sleeping"—have felt this influence, and acknowledged this power of Truth; and the Sacred Word itself—the foundation of Truth—is vastly indebted for its sublimity to the inspiration of the Poet.

In this age—practical, mechanical, and speculative beyond precedent—the bustle of commerce and the spread of enterprise have not been able to divert the public mind from the products of the imagination. Scotland is as proud of her large company of really gifted modern bards and versifiers as she is of her great and glorious roll of distinguished men of literature, science, philosophy, and invention. As children of the North, the names of our poets—Thomson, Scott, Burns, Campbell, Hogg, and a host of others—are known throughout the world. The same might be said in philosophy, of Hume, Stewart, and Macintosh; in science, of Playfair, Watt, and Leslie; in history, of Buchanan, Irvine, Gillies, M'Crie, and Alison; in criticism, of Jeffrey, Wilson, and Carlyle; in theology, of Knox, Blair, Chalmers, Irving, and Guthrie; in painting, of Ramsay, Raeburn, and Wilkie. As travellers, what brighter names are there than Park and Livingstone; in general literature, than Hugh Miller and Robert Chalmers. We have, in philological lore, the names of Chalmers and Jamieson, and in the mechanical arts time would fail us to speak of the Watts and Bells, and hundreds of other "Scots Worthies" to whose names our mills and factories and steam-shops are offering up continually their hoarse hymn of praise. But we have enumerated enough to prove that no country in proportion to its size has contributed so much as Scotland to the stock of intellectual wealth which is constantly accumulating in the world.

The lowly homes of Scotland—in rural retreats as well as in busy towns—have furnished a long list of honoured names that have shed a bright lustre over the walks of literature ; and no previous period of the world's history has produced so large a company of really gifted minor poets. In our work on "Modern Scottish Poets" we have seen that the minstrel breeze not only floats its music through the corridors of the palace, but also through the chinks and crannies of the cottage —flapping the tasselled curtains of the mansion, and even blowing in the rags which stuff the panes in the domiciles of squalor. Of our modern band of Scottish bards, the author of this volume is not the least true or the least tender amongst the sweet choristers.

John S. Rae was born on the 25th January, 1859—the hundredth anniversary of the birth of Burns—and was consequently ushered into the world amid a blaze of illuminations, and the general rejoicings of all Scotland, and her wandering sons "the wide warld ower." The place of his birth was an unpretentious farm-house at Cross Gight, New Deer, Aberdeenshire. Three or four years after the date of his birth his parents removed to Burngrains, Alvah, Banffshire, where they still reside. At an early age John devoured the chapman literature in which the north was so rich—warlike ballads and tender tales of love in "ye faire ladye's bowers." He still delights in tales of superstition, scraps of folk lore, and any anecdote illustrating our national peculiarities, and the study of such matters has given a rich, ballad tone to several of his poems and songs.

It was designed to make Mr Rae "a son of the soil," but holding the plough not being exactly suited to his frame of mind and body he resolved to try the wider fields of commerce. Accordingly he learned the drapery business, but only to find that life behind the counter was not so congenial to his taste as he had anticipated—his love of literature being still pre-eminent. However, he manfully toiled onwards. After being employed several years in Glasgow he removed to London, and entered one of the great wholesale houses. Delicate health, however, compelled our poet to leave London ; and again, through the same cause, and after being a few months in Dundee, he has had to return to his native Burngrains, hoping to recover his strength amid the beauties and salubrities of Nature.

He has cultivated with much success his favourite Muse in his spare moments after the bustling business of the day was over—

> A bardic son of commerce I,
> And here amid the strife
> Of cities with their turrets high,
> I note the tide of Life ;
> And on this tide the man must float
> Who lives amid the throng,
> With little time to raise the note
> Of sad or joyous song.

Many of the pieces that Mr Rae has given to the public through the medium of the newspaper press and literary ournals have met with a very favourable reception. In all these it is quite evident that he is a "Scotchman to the heel." There is a fine patriotic ring about his poems that relate to Scotland ; while those on the subject of his early home and youthful haunts are charmingly touching. The critical reader will doubtless find an occasional inequality, lack of finish, evidence of hasty writing, and passages where the realism is too pronounced, but will ever find present the cultivated taste. His poetical imagery is natural, pleasing, and singularly felicitous, giving evidence of the eye, the heart, the spirit, and the expression of the poet. His poems are the

effusions of an earnest heart—the truthful expressions of devotion to his kin and country, glowing word-pictures of brae-
sides, and happy sketches of the joys and sorrows of humble
life. He invests every spot and object around the home of
his youth with the charm of poetry, and finds in the beauteou
scenes of nature—the rich azure of the skies, the magnificence
of trees, and the retired haunts of the feathered songsters, as
well as in the melody of rivers, and in the sound of the wimpling burn,

> " That true delight
> Wealth cannot purchase, nor a sceptre yield."

To prove this, we might refer to many passages of much
sweetness ; but these cannot escape the most careless reader.
He finds the spirit of poetry by the couthie fireside, in the
London warehouse and the noisy workshop, amid the rustling
leaves in some fairy nook, or when whispering warm words
in the ear of some "kind dearie." Heart speaks to heart in
some of his tender love-words ; while in several of his poems
on city life, guilt and shame are depicted with startling vividness, and touching sorrow.

This volume gives evidence of versatility on the part of the
poet. We here find the sentimental, the patriotic, the humor-
ous, and the pathetic. We have the poetry of the individual
heart—its aspirings, its resolves, its hopes, and its fears ;—
the first swellings of youthful love that break forth in music,
the colours which lie in the enchanted distance, the secrets of
the trysting tree, the glad song of the bridal, the love of the
domestic circle, the parting embrace when the circle is first
broken, and the welcome return—all meet us here.

As we have already hinted, Mr Rae is imbued with great
national enthusiasm, and his thoughts often burn with noble
and patriotic aspirations, without affecting the mystical or
straining after mere ornate effect, while present-day topics
are treated with frank out-spokenness. He celebrates
with fire, spirit, and originality the fame of our ancient
warriors, knights, nobles, and ladies, reminding us that in the
middle ages the reigning idea of poetry was devotion to the

gentler sex, which, allying itself with martial fire, produced
what we call chivalry. It was then that the sword-point was
lowered at the glance of a bright eye ; and castles embosomed
in dark woods, terrific dragons, and superhuman beauties—all
that we mean by the word *romance*—these formed the staple
of the songs of the minstrels and troubadours.

We have referred to Mr Rae's "out-spokenness" on several
present-day topics, only a very few specimens of which appear here. The theme of a vigorous poem we have seen is the
interview of Andrew Melvin, James Melvin, and his cousin,
Thomas Buchanan, with George Buchanan—the Dr Johnson of
Scotland. Buchanan's "History of Scotland" appeared almost
the very moment of his death. Indeed, by the time the print-
ing was finished, and the work hailed with loud applause, the
soul of the historian was stepping into a grander theatre to re-
ceive " a Crown of Life." Buchanan showed them his dedica-
tion of the work to the King, and said he could make it no better,
having a higher business to attend to. He was asked what
that was. "To die," was the solemn answer. They went
thence to the printing-office to glance over the sheets of his
history. Finding an unguarded passage in reference to
Rizzio's funeral, they hurried back to remonstrate with the
author, whom they found now in bed. They told him the
expressions he used would anger the King, and perhaps lead
him to suppress the whole work. "Tell me, man," said
Buchanan, "if I have told the truth." "Undoubtedly, sir,"
replied his cousin. "Then," rejoined he, "I will abide his
feud, and all his kin's." Thus spoke the spirit of an ancient
Gael, and of one who, like John Knox, never feared the face
of man.

In our own age—from Burns to Tennyson—almost every
poet has sung of man as man, as deriving what honour he deserves from what is in his bosom, and not merely what is on
his back. It was our own peasant bard who first sang the
great song that voiced the glory of man as man, which had

been spoken of but never sung with real rapture till he poured forth the coronation ode—

> "A man's a man for a' that."

Tennyson is spoken of as the poet of ripe civilization. Although he writes for those of cultivated tastes, most of his heroes and heroines are the daughters of millers and gardeners, and the sorrows and resolves of a soldier are the subject of one of his most powerful poems. He thus acknowledges what makes all men of kin to him—the natural beating of the heart, the nobility of labour, and the might of individual effort. Thus he hails—

> "Men, my brothers ; men the workers,
>   Well I know
> That unto him who works, and feels he works,
> This same grand year is ever at the doors.

And our bard, too, in the present volume, in "Manhood," thus sings :—

> The fearless eye and forehead high,
>   The heart aglow with honour's soul—
> These are the marks of heraldry
>   That blazon Heaven's peerage roll—
> A chart whose lines divinely high
>   Outvie the world's most regal scroll.

Let us hope we are not many centuries away from the era thus prophesied by Mrs Browning :—

> "Drums and battle cries
> Go out in music of the morning star—
> And soon we shall have thinkers in the place
> Of fighters ; each found able as a man
> To strike electric influence through a race,
> Unstayed by city wall and barbican.
> The poet shall look grander in the face
> Than ever he looked of old, when he began
> To sing that Achillean wrath which slew
> So many heroes—seeing he shall treat
> The deeds of souls heroic towards the true."

November 1884.

POEMS AND SONGS.

—*✵✵*—

Scotia.

OF thee, O Scotia, would I fondly sing,
And pray the Muses for a time to fling
Their sacred shades across my humble way,
And tune my lyre to sing this rustic lay.
While all unworthy my untutored pen
To sketch the beauties of the hill and glen,
I pardon crave for this, myself, and Muse,
Which kindred Scots will surely ne'er refuse.

When patriot ardour in the bosom springs,
And unrestrained will touch the silent strings
Of musing fancy till they throbbing raise
Their voice impulsive in a song of praise,
Why should that bosom in its depths retain
The swelling cadence of the prompted strain?
'Tis better, surely, that its note should rise,
Though 't pass unheeded as an echo dies.

Such is my song, and such its fate may be,
I claim no merit from its measures free;
The honest Scot of independent mind
Who'd stoop for favour would disgrace his kind.
To Scots at home, and brother Scots away,
I humbly dedicate my simple lay,
And feel rewarded if this strain of mine
But wakes one memory of " Auld Lang Syne."

Sweet " Auld Lang Syne," thou dear familiar phrase,
The joys and sorrows of the bygone days
Rise at thy mention from the long ago,
And through the gates of memory surging flow.
The scenes that blest our youth rise up anew,
Old faces, mingled in the long review,
With forms beloved, mayhap long passed away,
That shone refulgent in our life's young day.

Thus " Auld Lang Syne" to Scots is ever dear,
And in their hearts they lovingly revere
Old Mother Scotia, first of lands on earth,
'Mid whose wild hills and lakes they had their birth.
How oft the wanderer on some distant shore
Draws sweetest solace from his dreams of yore,
When fancy lovingly doth homeward stray
Across the weary waste of watery way ;

And climbs once more the rugged mountain steep,
Thick dotted over with the bleating sheep,
And sees around the fields of yellow grain
With plenty crown the fertile spreading plain.
While sings the linnet 'mong the whin-clad braes
The song familiar to his early days,
When care was stranger to his boyish heart,
With all the sorrows that it can impart.

But swiftly sped those happy days along,
And youth soon ripened into manhood strong,
And brought the hour he said farewell to home
In climes far distant for a time to roam
In labour's mart with toiling hand to gain
The gold, perchance, for which he crossed the main,
Since independence is the dearest charm
That nerves to industry the freeman's arm.

Go range the globe, in climes of sun or snow,
You'll find your countrymen where'er you go

Still brave, unflinching, at their various posts,
In peace aye foremost as in war's red hosts.
Bravo! brave children of a noble land,
Ye are indeed a world-honoured band
In whom the virtues that our sires maintained
Shall live and flourish to the end unstained.

Each spot is sacred of the dear old land
That nursed and nourished the devoted band
Who bled for Scotland, for their homes and right,
And stood invincible 'gainst England's might.
The deeds of valour wrought by them of yore
Still live undying in tradition's lore ;
And while the thistle shall triumphant wave
The homes of Scotland shall uprear the brave.

For should the hour e'er wait upon her men
In arms to muster on the field again,
That hour should find them in their close array,
If danger loomed in golden freedom's way.
When cursèd bigotry with iron hand
Of old stalked rampant o'er the bleeding land
To crush pure worship with a tyrant rod,
And hush the praises of our sires to God ;

Each hill and glen by martyrs' blood besprent,
To hearts still faithful newer courage lent ;
The hunted preacher 'mid the wilds so drear
Still taught his followers the truths so dear ;
Then rose from silent glens the holy psalm,
Renewing fainting souls like precious balm ;
And fervent prayers on wings of faith arose
To Israel's God, to shield them from their foes.

He heard their voices ; and His mighty hand
Swept dark oppression from the groaning land,
And raised again His faithful from the mire,
Refined and purified, as gold by fire.

Is there a Scot whose bosom never thrills
With proud emotion as he scans those hills
That tower eternal with their peaks of snow,
And streams wild dashing to the glens below ?

Where lie the clachans and the cosy farms,
In beauty circled by their rural charms
'Mid sweet retreats where lovers fondly stray
When twilight dim bespeaks the closing day;
And far o'erhead the wheeling eagle screams,
While parting sunlight on his bosom gleams,
Revealing clear the mighty pinions sweep
That bear him swiftly to his mountain keep.

How oft of old those hills with battle rang,
And steel on steel with fiercest hate did clang,
When Scot met Scot, as Greek met Greek in war,
And sent the echoes of the fray afar.
Or when wild Dane or Norseman on our coasts
Did pour, to ravish with their dreaded hosts;
If those mute hills their secrets could upyield
They'd tell of many a carnage-covered field,

Where our brave sires with hearts and courage true
Did meet those rovers of the ocean blue,
And bear them down like sand before the tide,
While in their wake lay death and ruin wide.
The daring valour Scots of yore displayed
(Though great the odds they never were dismayed),
Still springs anew in each succeeding race,
And stamps its presence in each martial face.

On that dark morn of deadly Waterloo
Our gallant regiments, though in numbers few,
Hedged round with bayonets, stood each attack,
And hurled the mail-clad legions back.
Behold, the Cuirassiers in pride advance—
The chosen horsemen of the flower of France;

And hark! the thunder of the "Greys'" wild cheer,
Which tells the tyrant his defeat is near.

For swift as lightning on the French array
Down bore those troopers and their chargers grey,
And 'neath their swords the Cuirassiers went down
Like forest leaves when autumn winds are blown.
They who, amid an hundred fields' alarms,
Had proved their valour and their boasted arms,
And ne'er had charged but victory bore them through,
In death lay scattered now on Waterloo!

Beneath the deluge of that living flood
The star of victory did set in blood,
That led the conquering Napoleon on
O'er ravished empires to usurp a throne.
A hinge of destiny was that famed plain,—
The ghastly sepulchre of thousands slain,
Whose tale shall live in peaceful days to come,
When hushed for ever is the martial drum;

When warlike navies shall no longer sail,
Some coast to devastate with deadly hail;
When men shall blush to think the law of right
Their sires subverted to the law of might.
But we who flourish in this age must stand,
And ward oppression from our native land;
For still the wolf will make the lamb his prey,
As from the first of time hath been his way.

But clearly looms a-head that blissful time
When meek-eyed peace shall rule in every clime,
And nations, nobler grown, shall right decree
At honour's call with love and pleasure free.
Then shall the clarion of justice sound
This was her home when nations all around
Knew not the science of her golden rule,
For this brave Island was her early school.

The nations learned to venerate the might
We wielded only in the cause of right;
And tyrants shrank before our dreaded frown,
And licked the hand upraised to smite them down.
Imperial Cæsar in his greatest hour
Ne'er knew the glories of our honoured power;
In every land our flag hath been unfurled,
Our voices sway the councils of the world.

Far, where tho Himalays to heaven uprise,
Our sceptre rules beneath those arid skies;
Where graceful palms uplift their feathery arms,
And changing Nature showers her Orient charms;
And where Australia's fertile tracts expand,
With wealth of gold deep in her favoured land;
Where broad Pacific's glittering waves do roll
For many a league unbroken to their goal;

Where Afric's blazing sun darts scorching ray
On plain and swamp, and jungle's tangled way,
And spreading deserts, with their sands of fire,
Where Nature's self doth languish and expire.
Even there the children of our hardy land
Are toiling distant from their native strand;
But softer climes and skies of brighter blue
Can ne'er estrange them, Scotia dear, from you.

Ah! no, ah! no; where'er a Scot may roam
His heart unchanging ever turns to home;
Those sunny scenes that deck a brighter clime
But claim his fancy for a passing time.
The land of heather and of laughing rills,
The land of valleys and of towering hills,
Where sweet blue-bells and bearded thistles wave,
Alike the emblems of the fair and brave;

The land that's girded by the rolling deep,
Where liberty, enthroned on mountains steep,

Smiles down on fields deep furrowed by the free—
That is the land of every land for me.
Then let us pray that still the Powers above
May fan the flame of patriotic love,
And raise the warrior, the bard, and sage
To guide the people in each coming age.

Here noble Burns, king of bards, did reign,
And pour divinely his enchanting strain;
Still rolls the echo of his mighty song
The vasty corridors of time along.
His name, revered like quenchless beacon, glows,
And o'er the past a sacred halo throws,—
A household word all potent to impart
A thrill of pride to every Scottish heart.

The springing flowers recall his living name,
The wild birds pipe of his immortal fame,
And soft winds whisper as they steal along
Some fancied fragment of his magic song.
Now fiercely stern, anon his strain doth melt,
And breathe that tenderness and love he felt;
While laughing humour runs along his page,
With gravest thoughts all worthy of a sage.

He loved old Scotia, and he tuned his lyre
To sing her praise with true poetic fire;
Our homely Doric he has raised to fame—
'Twill live immortal with his lasting name.
And great Carlyle, the prophet and the sage,
The lettered genius of a lettered age,
His works, colossal as they are sublime,
Shall stand as monuments of worth through time.

He sleeps not proudly 'mong the gilded urns,
But rests obscurely, like his country's Burns,
In humble tomb—his noble mind but chose
A lowly place 'mong those from which he rose.

Oh! Scotia, sacred be the narrow bed
Which holds the ashes of thy mighty dead;
Thy prophet son his work hath ably done,
His task is over, and his laurels won.*

Well may a Scot with honour play his part,
While live those mem'ries in his inmost heart;
Well may he love his wild and northern home,
The best of lands wherever he may roam.
Domestic love sits by each lowly hearth,
Inweaving happiness with humble worth;
And sterling principles are early taught,
While yet young minds with innocence are fraught.

From sire to son each cherished tale descends,
And to the mind a noble impulse lends;
Upstirring there the old heroic fires
That shone so brilliant in our hardy sires.
Long may the heath wave purple on our hills,
Clear flow the currents of our silvery rills;
Bright be the blossom on the broomy braes,
Where birds pipe gaily through the summer days.

May modesty and grace adorn our maids,
And valiant manhood woo them in our glades;
And long the thistle with the rose entwine,
Both fraught *with memories of 'Auld Lang Syne.'*

Note.—The verses on Carlyle were inserted in the poem at the time of his death. The remainder of the poem was written about a year previous.

—◇—

Man Was Not Made to Mourn.

WHAT though thy feeble frame, O Man,
  By sorrow oft is torn,
    And Life seems but a dreary span—
    A trackless waste forlorn,
  Yet think not only to despair
    And trouble thou art born;
  'Tis vain to cull the roses fair
    And murmur at the thorn.

Look higher still beyond the mire
  Which clogs thy footsteps here,
And soon thine eye with brighter fire
  Shall glow divinely clear;
For though the Summer leaves may fall
  And flowers to ashes turn,
They spring anew at Nature's call
  And gaily earth adorn.

Out shame! upon the dwarfish minds
  That shrink from noble life;
Poor soulless ape is he that finds
  No pleasure in the strife.
With courage true stand in the lines
  Of higher life and spurn
The cynic who despairing whines
  That " Man was made to Mourn."

Up! mighty Man, assert thy power,
  And wrestle for the right,
Thy noble soul, great Heaven's dower,
  Shall bear thee in the fight;
For he that wills may vex his mind,
  No matter where he turn,
And sorrows not his own he'll find
  And o'er them pensive mourn.

Behold the twittering warblers gay
　Make vocal all the bowers,
Their happy hearts but pipe the lay
　That we restrain in ours;
The laverock high upon the wing,
　The blackbird on the thorn,
They but the song of Nature sing,
　Man was not made to morn.

Look round and mark the silent prints
　Of ages gone before,
A radiance from their pathway glints,
　Revealing men of yore,
Who tuned their chords in measures strong
　To cheer the heart forlorn,
And teach the sinking soul the song
　Man was not made to mourn;

And we who in these latter days
　No longer darkly grope,
But clearer see ahead the ways
　To pleasure peace and hope,
Know that the power which made us all
　Shall leave us not forlorn,
For He that notes the sparrow's fall
　Ne'er made Mankind to mourn.

The Holy Mills.

SOME preach because it is their trade,
　An' some by special callin',
　An' some because their lungs were made
For showman sort o' bawlin',

Some holy preachers act the priest
  By hecklin' an' by speirin',
Among the folk, frae west to east
  Aye constant interferin'.
Some ministers can sing a psalm,
  An' some can tell a story ;
An' some there are can tak' a dram
  As lang's its to the fore aye.
Auld Zion sits upon a hill,
  The State her seat supportin',
An' tak's a' grist into her mill,
  Wi' unco little sortin'.
She hauds on high her ancient flag—
  The Westminster Confession;
An' a' the corn in her bag
  Is gratis frae the nation.
Within her crap nae chuckie stanes
  Hae ever found a restin' ;
She feeds on beef, an' picks the banes
  To haud the lave frae tastin'.
The " Freemen " roun' aboot her pray,
  Her heathen state deplorin' ;
" She's dead asleep in sin," they say,
  An' swear they hear her snorin'.
But she's at heart a couthy dame,
  Although she's sair misca'd aye ;
An' though she's auld, she's nae sae lame—
  She is a supple jade aye.
The other Mills that roun' her stand
  By folks they're ca'd Dissentin';
Their wheels are heard a' owre the lan'
  Wi' din that's fair dementin'.
Nae fear there is that e'er their wheels
  Get time to stop an' freeze, O ;
For roun' them run a' kin' o' chiels,
  Aye haudin' in the greese, O.
They swear its purest oil o' faith

About their Mills they're pourin';
It maun be cheap, for by my aith
In floods they keep it stourin'.
An' some gang roun' at sic a rate
To winnow guid frae evil,
The chaff keeps fleein' ear' an' late
In clouds wad blin' the Devil.
Some think salvation comes to all
When they hae got a steepin',
Nae matter though they tak the caul',
A' shiverin' an' dreepin'.
These water billies think a chiel
Is better for the washin';
A guarantee against the deil
In future wi' him fashin'.
I doot it sair, for filth o' sin
Beneath the hide aye lies, O;
An' how they get the water in
My knowledge clean defies, O.
An' some believe that certain folks
For heaven are elected;
This doctrine may be orthodox,
But I wad hae't rejected.
It disna gang wi' common sense,
Nor does it fit wi' reason;
Although I may be tauld at once
That this is holy treason.
Auld Zion's Mill may need a men',
This truth I'm nae denyin',
But some hae need to sort their ain,
Wha holes in her are spyin'.
She is the root to ane an' a',
An' he's a shamefu' wether
Wha, when he's fit to box an' craw,
Wad turn against his mither.
The meal that's grun' at other mills,
Ca'd roun' wi' better water,

Should stap the mou's o' them it fills,
  An' lay their jealous clatter.
The Millers a' should mak a league
  To work beneath ae riggin'—
The Mills combined, the deil wad fleg
  Entirely frae the biggin'.
Then if the Pope should venture in,
  The holy Millers' quorum
Could throw the rascal i' the bin,
  An' there completely smore him.

—◇—

Winter.

THE skies are noo o' leaden hue,
  Wi' nae a tint o' azure blue
    In a' the scene,
An' bitin' showers go drivin' past
Upon the surly winter blast
    Sae chill an' keen.

The naked trees like spectres bare,
Noo stripped o' a' the glory fair
    O' summer gay,
Bend creakin' in the fitfu' gale
That 'mong the branches bleak doth wail
    A mournfu' lay.

'Tis Winter's dirge falls on the ear,
An' dark December's sough sae drear,
    Wi' eddyin' snaws,
Gars ilka creature seek some bield,
Themsel's frae Nature's wrath to shield
    Till it ower-blaws.

When cosy by the ingle cheek
Hoo' little do we ever reck
    O' beast an' bird
Exposed to Winter's wildest breath,
Which freezes them mayhap to death
    On the cauld yird.

Where are the birdies noo that sang
Sae sweet when summer days were lang,
    An' sunshine bright?
They piped their notes by stream and wood,
An' stirred the soul o' Bardic mood
    To poesy's flight.

In some bit neuk they'll be at rest,
For birds an' beasts are guided best
    By Instinct's law,
An' He will sure for them provide
Whose hand controls the wind an' tide,
    An' gently guides us a'.

The wanderin' poor wha hae nae hame,
When they thy help an' pity claim,
    O'erlook them not;
Ye wha wi' goods are favour'd well
Hear not wi' sneers their wofu' tale,
    Nor scorn their lot,

But gie according as you're bless't
Wi' plenteous store, you'll never miss't,
    An' when you're gone
Those kindly deeds will pass before,
An' help to open Heaven's door,
    An' sins atone.

True charity, an' kindly word
Will hae their due an' full reward—
    Sae Scripture says;

An' he wha helps a fellow man
Wi' generous heart surpasses one
    Wha graspin' prays.

O ! ye wha wear deceitfu' mask,
An' in the sun o' favour bask
    Wi' Kirk an' State,
Just call poor Lazarus' case to mind,
Wha helpless lay distress'd, we find
    At rich man's gate ;

An' he wha was sae grand arrayed,
His deeds when in the balance weighed
    Were found to fail,
Nor could his sumptuous riches save
Him from destruction an' the grave,—
    His end was Hell.

An' think not that the changing age
Can blot the record of that page,
    Nor right abate,
For Heaven high to great an' sma',
Gie's the same universal law
    And entrance gate.

—◇—

Manhood.

" An honest man's the noblest work of God."

A BARD am I whose highest thought
    Is centred in the wish sublime,
    Some goodly influence to have wrought
For humankind of every clime—
Some effort lasting as the years,
    To teach them truly what they are—

Some balm to give to stay earth's tears,
   Till eyes grow bright as morning star,
And gloom and doubt and rending fear
   Are banished 'yond life's ocean bar.

When passion's power hath had its hour,
   And crumbled is this frame of clay,
Man's soul shall wield a grander power
   Beyond the span of mortal day.
Then live, my brother, not as tho'
   The present time were all to thee,
Those hours of life are but the glow
   Of dawn to thy eternity,—
Fear man nor fiend, to God but bow,
   He gave thy life and thou art free.

Behold the tyrant, see him rise
   A slave to fierce malignant will,
The darkling glare within whose eyes
   Might light some dusky cave of hell.
Stand not afar in abject fear,
   Nor trembling meet his scowling face,
But mock his threats with calmest sneer,
   And dare the villain of thy race
With manly eye serene and clear,
   As thou would'st brave some beast of chase.

When ravening wolves harass the fold,
   How swift at morn or night or noon
The watchman meets th' invaders bold,
   And deals his vengeance sharp and soon;
And why should beasts in human guise
   Through years harass the race of man?
The blame with you my brothers lie,
   Whose Heavenly guerdon everyone
Is liberty, right to defy
   The tyrant wretch and live say I,

So that as one great camp, the earth
  In peace and plenty may repose,
And strife and envy banished forth
  Shall leave your life a thornless rose
Within a fair and radiant clime,
  Whose air for ever feeds its bloom
Through all the circling change of time
  'Neath skies that know·no cloud of gloom;
Who makes of life this scene sublime
  Can never know oblivion's tomb.

No mortal unit can alone
  This empire of the earth create,
Thus none are worthy of the throne
  To singly rule this mighty State,
But hand in hand with hearts agreed
  Let humankind together draw
The chart by which they will be freed,
  And frame in peace the golden law
Of Brotherhood, whose precious seed
  Each fellowman hath power to sow.

The poorest of the earthly poor,
  If they but own a noble mind,
Hath lineage and rank more pure
  Than all the kings of humankind.
The fearless eye and forehead high,
  The heart aglow with honour's soul,
These are the marks of heraldry
  That blazon Heaven's peerage roll,
A chart whose lines divinely high
  Outvie the world's most regal scroll.

I'd rather be an honest man,
  And honest poverty my share,
Than be a lord and bear the ban
  Of hollow-hearted mammon fair,
C

If allied with a barren brow,
    And heart's unsympathetic chord;
An empty name it is I trow
    To be a mindless titled lord,
And like a drone to live, I vow,
    Upon an ill-begotten hord.

That one who thrills the chords of life,
    Who gives the aching bosom rest,
And stills the rancorous tongues of strife,
    Is surely to be loved and bless'd.
Where such there is, then such a one,
    Though poor and meek, obscure from fame,
Stand proudly up thou art a Man,
    And worthy of the noble name—
A leader in the world's van,
    True earner of a diadem !

Let such a one stand forth, say I,
    And cast his seed on every breeze,
And sowing let him sing full high
    Strong songs to elevate and please
His toiling brothers far and wide,
    Till earth its rivers, hills, and seas
Are vocal with the notes that glide
    Like murmurs 'mong the forest trees,
Soft floating far on echoing tide,
    Of strange and wondrous melodies,
Till countless throats sing this refrain
    In Hope's prophetic mystic strain :

HOPE'S PROPHETIC SONG.

I can see far down the vista
    Of the years that are to be,
From the womb of time come trooping
    Forth a mighty race and free

To a higher field of labour,
  To a vantage ground of fight;
On their brows a nobler manhood,
  In their eyes a purer light.

They will scan the misty records
  Of the ages left behind,
Adding lore of Greek and Roman
  To their miracle of mind.
With their march still on and upward
  Till they blend the god in man
I can see them nobly fighting
  In the world's serried van;

And the powers now hid in darkness
  They will bring forth to the light,
And shall gird them with their knowledge
  In one Brotherhood of might,—
Shaping all things to their uses
  Till they reach the golden goal,
When the man shall stand triumphant,
  Worthy of his mighty Soul.

Then the world's song of victory
  In a Pæan grand shall rise—
In one noble swelling chorus
  From the nations to the skies.
Fellow-workers labour onward,
  Nearer, clearer, shines the light
Of that glorious day, whose dawning
  Shall dispel the world's night.

Yule Night.

[The ancient custom of observing Yule-Tide, once so popular in Scotland, is now almost extinct, except in some of the northern counties, and even there it is fast becoming a relic of the times that were. It was customary among the peasantry on this night to convene to drink "sowens," which is the juice or "bree" of the outer shell of the corn after being ground for meal. On these occasions dancing, singing, and legendary lore made up the simple programme of rustic amusement.]

'TIS merry Yule, and fu' o' glee,
　　The folks convene to haud a spree,
　　　　An' hae a jolly splore,
Just as their fathers aye hae done,
For weel they relished mirth an' fun
　　　　In happy days o' yore.

This nicht the famous sowen bree
Is ladled oot wi' measure free
　　　　In dishes big an' sma',—
A mellow, liquid feast sae gran',
Peculiar to oor northern lan'
　　　　O Spartan stamachs a'.

Ben in the neuk the orra loon
The fiddle scraips an' puts in tune
　　　　Wi' great palaver sair,
An' aye he gies some pin a screw,
An' rosins up the bow anew,
　　　　Wi' muckle skill an' care.

The best o' fiddlers roun' an' roun',
Without a doubt's the orra loon,
　　　　He beats a' rivals clean.
Wi' haughty scorn o' other's ways
He grips the bow, an' wildly plays
　　　　Wi' native genius keen.

Noo he has got it richt at last,
An' wi' the dancers trippin' fast
　　　　The very rafters ring ;

An' 'mid the capers and career
That stirring Scottish tune I hear—
   Ca'd " Huntly's Heilan' Fling,"

The " Brig o' Banff," the " Braes o' Mar,"
An' lilts that stir in peace or war
   Are fiddled ane an' a',
Till e'en the auldest folks grow fain
To wish for supple shanks again
   In spite o' Nature's law.

An' sangs are sung an' stories tauld,
While fast the nicht is wearin' auld,
   Unnoticed 'mid the fun,
For lads an' lasses when they meet
Nae heed they gie to time sae fleet—
   The hours like minutes run.

Lang cherished by those rural ways—
The relics o' departed days,
   Inwoven wi' the fame,
Oor fathers won in years gone by,
Sae let their memory never die
   While Scotland bears its name.

—◇—

The Minstrel.

A WANDERER of the minstrel train,
   With ancient garb and locks of grey,
     Stood 'mid the hushed and listening throng,
   Which paused as he began to play.

His eyes did glisten as his hand
   Swept swiftly o'er the wonderous thing
That poured the gushing sounds so sweet,
   Like angel voice it seemed to sing.

Upon the busy street he stood,
  While rose the swelling music sweet
In wildly thrilling magic strains
  Above the din of hurrying feet.

Now Spring seemed in each warbled note,
  With greening groves and springing flowers,
As bird-like forth the music streamed
  Like echoes from the woodland bowers.

Then Summer's sultry skies seemed near,
  With lightning's flash and thunder's roll,
While soft and airy zephyrs rose
  And winged around the raptured soul.

And Autumn's hollow winds would sigh,
  And shower the fading forest leaves;
Anon the changing strain would seem
  The rustling grain in golden sheaves.

Then wintry blasts with dreary moan,
  And silvery sledge-bells tinkling near
In bursts of grandest music fell
  Upon the listening ravished ear.

That wonderous power, immortal dower,
  Which gave the minstrel's hand its skill
To thrill the heart and move the soul,
  Obedient to the wanderer's will

Threw over all a magic spell
  Who heard those strains divinely sweet,
In measured melody that rose,
  And stayed the busy passer's feet.

The minstrel ceased, and with the throng
  He mingled as he moved away;—
I look in vain for him again,
  With ancient garb and locks of gray.

London.

HAIL, London! "Babylon" of modern times,
Let great St Paul's ring out its wonderous
chimes
In giant notes of mighty melody,
Grand waves of music o'er a human sea,
For lo! a singer of these latter days
Now lifts his voice amid thy mighty maze
To sing thy glories and thy sombre gloom,
Thou seat of revelry and living tomb.
There's magic, London, in thy regal name;
O! City vast, thy glory and thy fame
Have travelled far to Earth's remotest bound
Where'er the pulse of human life is found.
When Rome in ages that have passed away,
O'er infant England held Imperial sway,
The native huts that straggled o'er thy site
Were they the shadows of thy coming might?
And could a Roman in his martial pride
Have drawn time's veil inscrutable aside,
And viewed the London of this later time—
A great Metropolis to every clime.
Had he beheld the ceaseless human tide
That flows and surges like an ocean wide,
And heard the wheels of traffic's golden car
Like thunder rolling ever near and far,
His soul, amazed, had leapt with wonder's thrill
As at the moving of a "magic spell,"
And all the visions of a Cæsar's might
Waned from his mind like stars 'fore morning light.

See, great *St Stephen's first arrests the eye,
Its towers majestic and its turrets high;
Their gilded spires shoot upward as to shade
The grey old Abbey and its mighty dead.

' Houses of Parliament.

There sits the Parliament whose sovereign hand
Gives law and equity to all the land,
Whose voice 'mong nations is a sound revered,
And by the enemies of freedom feared.
This high assembly of the noblest worth
Is Britain's pride, and famed throughout the earth;
The people's will is represented there,
And liberty and right sit mated pair.
In bygone days the Tories and the Whigs
In antique garments and in powdered wigs,
Awoke the echoes of those mighty halls
With sturdy argument and party brawls.
The noble leaders in the mental fray
Have lived and died and passed from us away,
But name and fame in history survive,
And yet, though dead, those heroes are alive.
The Pitts, the Foxes, and the Peels are gone,
Those mighty orators that brilliant shone;
They fought for Britain, and their bloodless war
Of all her victories the noblest are.
But later times have brought us names renowned—
A witty Beaconsfield with honours crowned,
A mighty Gladstone with a giant power
Of noble intellect as Nature's dower,
And honest Bright with flag of peace unfurled,
He preaches freedom to the list'ning world,
Free trade and liberty to every land,
This is the motto of the Quaker grand.
Such are the men whose eloquence has shed
A fadeless lustre on Britannia's head,
Whose lasting " footprints on the sands of time "
Shall guide our nation to its goal sublime.

But leave not Westminster till we have seen
The grey old Abbey and its niches green,
Those silent tombs ye Britons all revere,
Our nation's mightiest and best are here.

Her warrior sons, their victories all past,
In this famed cemetery repose at last,
'Mid mourning pageants and Britannia's tears
Fame laid them lowly on their honoured biers.
Some fell in glory on our fields afar
'Mid charging squadrons and the clash of war,
And on our decks some fell amid the fray
When Britain's " tars " to triumph fought their way.
At duty's post they bravely took their stand,
And fell unflinching with the sword in hand ;
Thus fell brave Nelson 'mid the battle's roar,
He'll steer to fame our " wooden walls " no more.
He rests not here, but tranquilly he lies
By noble Wellington, the great and wise ;
Beneath St Paul's revered and sacred shade
Their honoured bones in brotherhood are laid.
The roll of drums and tread of martial feet
To " Iron " Wellington was music sweet,
The glittering bayonets and the columns wide
Imbued his bosom with a patriot pride.
Shall Britain's greatness or her glory fade,
Tho' those bright ones are numbered with the dead ?
Do not their memories and deeds survive
And stir their countrymen to nobly strive,
And work as patriots in every field,
Whate'er the weapon 'tis their lot to wield,
With heart and will till victories are won,
And honoured laurels lie their brows upon.
From tombs of fame doth inspiration spring,
That fires the patriot to war or sing,
Or raise his voice 'mid legislation's throng,
To strengthen justice and to censure wrong.
The years are pregnant with the germs of strife—
Such wars as meet us in our daily life,
And shades of heroes from the past wave on
Stout hearts to battle in life's Marathon.

Advance the banners then of civil fray,
Ye leaders valiant of the ranks to-day
Fight strong and well each nobly as he can,
To make a pathway for the world's van.
In "Poet's Corner" of this hallowed glade
The Muse's votaries of song are laid,
Whose noble thoughts from heaven-inspired pen
Flowed forth to teach and charm their fellow-men,
Their's was the art to flash the flowing rhyme
In golden numbers from their lyres sublime,
To please the ear and educate the heart,
And lofty sentiment to all impart.
But other scenes, alas! and other sounds,
Are found, great Babylon, within thy bounds—
Where wealth and worth and nobleness all flower,
There too doth misery and vice uptower.
The hollow thrones of folly and of pride
In fashion's halls rise gaily side by side,
And thousands flutter in those gilded bowers,
Where health and sustenance decay like flowers.
Exalted Vice her gaudy chariot drives
'Mong wrecks deplorable of ruined lives
That woo'd her once with fortune in their hand
And drove her gaily through the brilliant Strand.
At Drury Lane in boxes highest priced
They viewed the drama and had vintage iced,
While scented fans drove airy cyclones rare
'Mong eye-glassed beaux and powdered maidens fair.
Or at the Lyceum of tragic fame
Frequented nightly by the London créme,
They ogled Irving as he strode the stage,
The king of actors of the present age.
Aglow with diamonds, rings, and jewels—
The lavish ornaments of monied fools,
Gay pleasure's votaries they had their swing
For a brief time ere shuffled from the ring;
For vicious folly had their purses reft

Of all they'd gained, or luckily been left
By some relation who, thro' virtuous life
And ceaseless industry in business strife,
Had lived in comfort and his needs supplied,
Then willed the surplus to his friends, and died.

Who that has wandered in the great West End,
Where London grandees with their stiffness lend
An air that's regal to the famous "Row,"
But well remembers of the costly show,
When vanity and rank vied each with each
Great fashion's lessons to the mob to teach,
Parading milliners' and tailors' skill,
But hiding carefully the unpaid bill.
Of course they were not all of this degree,
Some were real turtle in entirety ;
And Wests and Langtrys as the reigning belles
Swelled up the ranks of sounding titled " swells."
The wealthy merchant in the City bred,
Is now an alderman, and aims to wed
His charming daughter to an Earl's son
Who dangles after her for wicked fun.
The brilliant ball-room and its waxy floor,
With Amouretta how he trips it o'er,
And many a squeeze in secret he has given,
That made his lady love feel half in heaven.

Ah ! mighty London could the world see
Beneath thy guise of pleasant gaiety,
Or know the springs of sorrow's bitter tears,
That flow forever thro' the weary years.
Could I lay bare the deep philosophy
Of all the movings of that human sea !
This rare old world would stop in sheer amaze,
Or break its axis in a startled craze.

Jock o' Heather-Faulds.

THE famous market toon o' Turra,
    A risin', thrivin', thrifty burgh,
      Kent far an' near for pork an' leather
An' cooncillors that fecht thegither,
Ae nicht beheld a fearsome scene,
The like o' which has never been;
But this the subject o' my tale
To show in rhyme what here befell.
For drunken Jock o' Heather-Faulds
That day had sell't his twa-year-aulds,
An' ower the sellin' o' the stots
Had filled his pouches weel wi' notes.
Noo Jock could ne'er conclude a bargain—
Nae e'en for drainin' or for dargin'—
But owre it he wad hae a drappie
To keep his wame an' wizzen sappie;
An' mair especially on a day
That fortune blew the win' his way
Did Jock delight to draw the cork,
An' set the wheels o' fun to work.
At cattle markets, trysts, an' roups
His average was a dizen stoups,
But when the win' was i' the east
He aften took a score at least,
To kill the cauld an' raise the heat,
An' ease the corns upon his feet;
An' though he was a grippy chiel
The drouthy birkies kent him weel,
An' i' the Black Bull aften met
Wi' him to hae a whisky spate.
Sae on this nicht o' which I speak,
Half hid wi' pipe an' toddy reek,
Jock an' his cronies sat thegither,
An' gleyed an' blinked at ane anither,
While empty stoups an' glasses rang

Upon the board wi' mony a bang.
A sma' affair when men are bousin'
Is aft the theme o' muckle newsin',
Sae on this nicht, frae drunken toasts
The subject changed to deils an' ghosts,
An' Jock, wha had the " Horseman Word,"
Declared fu' stoutly by the Lord
That he had seen baith ghosts and deevil
An' haill machinery o' evil.
His cronies mutely sat wi' fear,
Prepared some awfu' tale to hear,
As he began, wi' solemn face,
To gi'e partic'lars o' the case.
Ae market nicht, 'twas gey an' late—
Weel on to twal at onyrate—
When canterin' hame frae Muir o' Ord,
As sober as a judge or lord,
He saw approachin' frae a' airts
What seemed to him like strings o' cairts ;
But what was maist infernal queer,
Nae soun' o' wheels cam' to his ear.
His frichtened mare began to swerve,
Although a beast o' powerfu' nerve,
An' like a tottum whirlin' roun'
She heaved him clean upon his croon.
A thousan' sparks flew in his sicht
Like shootin' stars in wintry nicht,
An' when he sprachled to his feet
A fearsome sicht his orbs did meet.
His guid auld mare, like flash o' licht,
Was disappearin' fast frae sicht ;
While roun' him, close on ilka han',
A thousan' hearses took their stan',
Wi' each upon't a grinnin' figure
As black an' grim as ony nigger.
Frae oot the hearses bodies crowded,
In sheets o' linen wrapped an' shrouded,

Wi' een like ghastly stars that burned,
As in their sockets lean they turned ;
While maiths an' worms an' giant fleas
Upon them crawled as thick as bees.
Jock's fear, my words are weak to paint it ;—
He roared aloud an' nearly faintet,
An' syne he tried a prayer to soun'
His mither learned him when a loon,
But deil ae word did he noo mind o't
Except the ane just at the end o't,
Yet, better that, thocht Jock, than nane,
As solemnly he gasped—*Amen !*
Auld Nick himsel' at last appeared,
An' through the corpses wild careered,
Wi' mony a fiendish howl an' yell,
Like echoes frae the vaults o' hell.
He looked a weird an' monster brute
O' sooty hue frae head to foot,
As hairy as a heilan' stot,
Or shaggy bearded billygoat.
He waved aloft a flamin' cowe
O' whin, that shed a flarin' lowe
Amang the ranks he capered through
At this grim midnicht hour review.
Attendant devils here an' there
As sentries travelled pair an' pair
Around the silent host o' dead
Thus mustered for the deil's parade.
At signal frae their sable lord,
The silent ranks with one accord
Began to madly dance an' shout,
An' throw the loathsome worms about.
They grinned in ane anither's faces,
An' tore an' tugged at ither's dresses,
An' kicked an' sprauled an' boxed an' battled,
Till banes an' joints like pea-cods rattled.
Thus, roun' an' roun', they ran fu' nackie,

Like idle loons when playin' tackie,
Syne fell on Jock, wi' fiendish glee,
And dragged him through the wild meleê.
In vain he roared, his mou' they stappit,
An' in a hearse his body clappit—
A hearse that smelt o' coffins mony,—
Then a' was owre wi' drucken Johnny.
He kent nae mair, till on the morn,
Wi' dubby claes an' breeks a' torn,
He wakened, wi' an achin' croon,
Just where auld Susie threw him doon.
Amazed wi' fear, his cronies pale
Had hearkened to the dismal tale;
Nae single word they dared to speak,
An' ilka pipe had ceased to reek.
Yet still they sat aroun' the board
And glowered, but uttered not a word,
Till Jock mistook their fear for doubt,
An' roused them wi' an angry shout,
An' struck the table wi' sic bang
That jugs an' glasses reeled an' rang,
As oot he bellowed wi' an aith—
It's fact, as sure's I draw my breath.
Again the social pipe was lit,
An' confidence began to sit
Ance mair on ilka merry wight
That late sat dumb wi' awesome fright,
An' pleasure took her throne again
Amid a circle a' her ain,
Whase sangs an' jokes an' stories droll,
Wi' humour pregnant, stormed the soul
O' ilka chiel, wi' rantin' roar,
That shook the gravest to the core.
But Father Time, the tireless loon,
By day an' nicht keeps movin' roun'—
Nae power o' human art an' skeel
Can ever clog the rascal's wheel.

Alike in hours o' woe an' mirth,
At funeral, wedding, an' at birth,
The human race may creep or hurry,
But time they canna stay nor flurry.
When noddin' owre the frien'ly bowl,
The clay-encircled human soul
Its earthly sark may throw aside
An' reck a while for time nor tide ;
But short an' fleetin' is the pleasure
That springs frae Bacchus' brimming measure,
Like glory's grandest, proudest flashes,
A minute's blaze expires in ashes.
But leavin' sarks an' souls an' glory
As subjects for some ither story,
We'll cast oor e'e again on Jock,
Wha's noo as fou's a puddin' pock,
" The malt was fairly owre the meal,"
An' wi' a rare domestic zeal,
Just as the clock, wi' whirrin' clang,
The fatal hour* to drinkers rang,
He slittered up to mak' for hame,
To soothe his irefu' waitin' dame.
Experience taught him weel the lesson
O' Maggie's wrathfu' curtain dressin',
An' hoo ae nicht, when late he cam',
As usual fuddled wi' a dram,
His angry wife, wi' scold an' clatter,
Had ducked him in a tub o' water,
Till ilka limb did shake an' shiver,
An' he had sworn to be for ever
The chief o' decent sober men,
An' ne'er bide drinkin' late again.
This vow he made wi' hideous wail,
As splashin' like an arctic whale
He kicked the tub an' Maggie o'er,
An' flooded a' the kitchen floor.

* Eleven o'clock

Then cam' Mackenzie's closin' ack,
The cooncils o' the wife to back,
An' gar't the public-hooses lock
Their doors at sharp eleven o'clock.
Nae langer owre the social drappie
May bousers sit an' tipple happy,
Till early streaks o' mornin' grey
Bespeak anither mortal day.
Oor ancient sires were canny men,
An' aye full weel could haud their ain,
The Kirk an' State they baith revered,
An' hated folks that interfered.
They liked 'mang flo'ers the rose sae white—
The emblem o' the Jacobite—
An' wi' it planted side by side
The sturdy thrissle, Scotland's pride.
But things hae altered in oor day,
The relics auld are swept away,
We're wiser in oor generation,
Sae things hae got a reformation.
But Jock at last has mounted Susie,
Wha kens fu' weel when he is bousie,
An' wadna start until he's siccar, ·
Syne aff she canters wi' a niccar.
By Hutcheon's shop an' doon the street,
The trusty mare was trottin' fleet,
But, as she neared the auld kirkyard,
Jock reined her up fu' sharp an' hard.
His phantom-teemin' brain that nicht
Was workin' wonders wi' his sicht,
For there he saw wi', awesome dread,
The opening graves gie up their dead.
Like owls or bats the ghostly people
Were clusterin' roun' the auld kirk steeple,
An' on the headstanes an' the dykes
They swarmed as thick as bees in bykes.
Oh! climax o' a' earthly wunners,

D

To see the dead rise up in hunners !
Jock's verra hair, like palin' posts,
Stude up on en' to see the ghosts !
Wha's fiery een, wi' demon licht,
Were glowerin' at him thro' the nicht ;
An' when he heard a hollow hummin',
An' thocht the haill brigade was comin',
He dashed the spurs into his mare,
An' closed his een in wild despair,
And darted by the fatal spot
Wi' whizzin' soun' like cannon shot.
He skelpit through the " Howe o' Hell "*
As if Auld Nick were at his tail
Wi' a' the speerits oot o' grace
Pell-mell ahin' him in the chase.
Wi' hoofs resoundin' on the grun',
Sae fast an' hard did Susie run,
That doors an' windows fairly shook,
Till frightened folks the soun' mistook
For some impondin' danger near,
An' groaned aloud wi' mortal fear ;
But Jock, without a thocht or notion
O' makin' sic a dread commotion,
Tore wildly on wi' reckless rattle,
As fierce dragoon darts on to battle.
Up Castlehill an' roun' the neuk
He dashed as quick as e'e could look,
His coat-tails oot ahint him streamin',
An' in each pouch a bottle gleamin'.
At ilka lash his startled mare
Like rabbit jumpit i' the air
Wi' frantic motions, wild an' free,
As, like a craw, she tried to flee.
Thus urged along poor Susie danced
An' reared an' plunged an' madly pranced,

---

* " Howe o' Hell," a well-known part in Turriff, nearby the Auld Kirk,
which is now a ruin.

While in his seat Jock tossed and swayed
Like thrissle tap or dockin blade.
Great po'ers! it was a wondrous sicht
To see him grippin', main an' micht,
Wi' baith his han's, to mare an' saddle,
Wi' motions like a " Coup the ladle,"
While at ilk caper, sway, an' swither
The bottles clanged an' banged thegither.
But fast an' faster noo they spin
Like desert dust afore the win',
Across the brig, owre Deveron's floods,
Alang the road by Forglen's woods,
An' up by Kirkton at the gallop,
Wi' mony a savage crack an' wallop
Upon puir Susie's reekin' hide,
To urge her faster still to stride,
For Jock, wha dared not look ahin',
Thocht ilka sough o' tree an' win'
Betokened that the ghostly crew
Had him and Susie still in view.
His heart wi' fear was loupin high
As lonely woods he darted by,
An' owls an' cushies screamed an' flappit,
Till frae his mare he nearly drappit.
Wi' fervent hopes o' preservation
Frae ghosts an' a' his tribulation,
Jock muttered aft this nicht again
His only prayer—Amen! Amen!
An' vowed if only hame ance mair
He ne'er wad bide at roup or fair,
As he had done this nicht sae late,
Till ghosts an' deils his road beset.
Lang after this, wi' bated breath,
Jock tauld, wi' mony a solemn aith,
How on this nicht the Turra ghosts
Pursued him hame in howling hosts.
He galloped o'er the darksome miles,

An' hedges, ditches, dykes, an' stiles
The supple Susie nimbly cleared,
As Heather-Faulds at last they neared.
Jock ne'er forgot his fleg that nicht—
His hair an' beard grew grey wi' fricht,
An' when he ventures noo frae hame
His loving Maggie, prudent dame,
Can mark, wi' smile o' joyfu' woman,
Her sober lord on Susie comin',
Ere gloamin' fa', frae toon or burgh,
For weel he minds his trot frae Turra.

—◇—

Vanity Fair.

(A BALLAD FOR THE TIMES.)

WHEN first into this Fair I went,
    All men alike I deemed,
        And took for granted that all things
Were truly what they seemed.

But ere I far into this Fair
    My youthful way had ranged,
Alas! by sad experience,
    My notions soon were changed.

For what I took for solid gold
    I found was often brass,
And when I thought I had a horse
    I oftener had an ass.

I'd hail a seeming honest face,
    My way about to ask,

But found ere I had spoken long
  Sir Honest wore a mask.

'Mong mingled doctrines here I found
  One Gospel take the van,—
'Twas gather cash by every means,
  And gull your fellow-man.

And to this end the stalls were set,
  All in a gaudy row,
Piled high with many a glittering ware
  To help the hollow show.

The venders, shouting loud and long,
  In trumpet-tones announced
That what they sold was sold at cost—
  All profits they renounced.

If this were so, how could they live,
  And pay an honest pound ?
The tale was no reality,
  But pure and simple sound.

I saw the May-Fair* carriages
  Wheel by in gilded line,
Their owners nigh invisible
  'Neath glitter and 'neath shine;

On eyes that Nature gave them,
  They fastened bits of glass,
And, monkey-like, they squinted
  When simpler folks would pass.

At billiards and at bagatelle,
  The turf, the cards, and dice,
Those glass-eyed gentry waste their time
  And money in a trice ;

* May-Fair, an aristocratic district of London.

Or lounging at gay liquor-bars,
  Where foreign maids preside,
They whisper love o'er brandy
  And virtuous tales confide!

In restaurants and cafés
  They guzzle, strut, and stare,
And chew their silver-headed canes
  To show they have them there.

No matter that some pious friends
  Have oft to pay some bill
To save their youthful progeny
  From Newgate's grimy jail.

Those youthful birds, ere feathered full,
  Their flights must still increase,
And so they quacking join the throng
  Of older, wilder geese,

Composed, of course, of gentlemen,
  Gay military swells,
Ignoble lords, and shoddy dukes,
  And well-rung city belles.

A Frenchman when in Paris
  Can gaily play the fool,
But go to mighty London
  And study "Johnnie Bull."

E'en "Sandy," though he's credited
  With common sense the best,
There joins, to play the frivolous,
  And crack a wicked jest.

Our covenanting ancestors
  Would scowl with heavy frowns

Were they to see the antics now
That grace our modern towns.

The thunders of a second Knox
Might have more weight than rhymes
To controvert the evils and
Abuses of the times.

That powerful goddess, Fashion, rules
The destinies of man,
And in this Fair of Vanity
All worship her who can.

Poor Israel in the wilderness
To golden calf did bow,
But modern Britain pitiful
Bends to a golden cow.

Our beaux and belles from novelettes
Derive their mental food—
Bright butterflies of literature
That teach a world of good.

Alas! for deep Philosophy,
Entomed it hidden lies;
And Poetry, all æsthetical,
Is valued by its sighs!

The Bible, good and ancient book,
Is counted as a bore,
Because it mentions not the cut
Of trousers Adam wore;

Nor does it tell the length of robe,
The style and colour chaste,
That decked our simple mother Eve
When first her form was dressed.

Great banks and speculations big
   On credit rise and fall,
And throw the golden millions round
   As boys would a ball.

No matter though the cash be lost,
   There's more where it came from,—
'Twill only mean to managers
   Some months in a new home.*

Released from jail, they're back again
   At speculation's game,
And should they win instead of lose
   It brings them wealth and fame.

The world applauds the clever rogue
   That swindles millions rife,
But hoots the poor and hungry wretch
   Who steals to save his life.

Here in this Fair are merry maids
   Well versed in folly's rules,
To buy whose charms some princes gay
   Ere now have pawned their jewels.

Bewitched by wine and harlots fair
   A certain royal clown,
Once chief of many an amour,
   Nigh pawned the British Crown,

And left some handsome legacies
   For poorer folks to pay,
Which oathless Charlie Bradlaugh
   Would fairly sweep away.

Oh! that "Perpetual Pension" list
   Deserves our due regard ;

---

* Perth Prison, for example.

It tells how ancient virtue was,
    As now, " its own reward."

E'en Solomon, that king of kings
    For wisdom and for lore,
When in this Fair of Vanity,
    Had darlings by the score.

Full many a pair of pouting lips
    Were waiting at his call,
And truth to tell I pity him
    Ere he had kissed them all!

But thus it is the world goes on,
    And still the hollow show
Attracts the crowd, as candle doth
    The moth by brilliant glow.

The holy monk, in convent cell,
    Prays for the world's good,
But is he a true champion,
    And acting as he should?

Why wastes he thus the precious hours
    Apart from this great Fair,
His sphere for real and honest good
    Is 'mong the millions there.

To battle with the tide of time
    One needs must stem the stream,
Instead of resting on its banks
    Among the flowers to dream.

All hollow sham and mockery,
    All shoddy show and gloss
Is but a weak philosophy—
    At best a heap of dross.

Put down the cant, the show, and sham,
 My honest friends eachwhere,
And spurn away the gilded dross,
 The hollow empty glare,

Till honest action lifts its head
 And proves the morning star
To usher in that glorious day
 That shows things as they are.

Then may the simple and the wise
 Preambulate life's fair
With honest hearts 'mong honest men
 That deal in honest ware.

---◇---

Jeanie.

A BALLAD OF SAUCHIEBURN.

IN olden times, when mailèd knights
 Wi' sword gied Scotland law,
 There dwelt a winsome ladye fair
At Elden-Thristle Ha',
Young Jamie was a border knight
 An' mony a fray had seen,
And dearly lo'ed wi' a' his heart
 Brave Elden-Thristle's Jean,
An' bricht an' bonnie 'tween the twa
 The love-rose red grew fair,
Till Sauchieburn's fatal field
 Brocht dool an' woe fu' sair.
Young Jamie had to leave his love
 An' sairly did she mourn,
But little thocht he'd ne'er come back
 Frae fatal Sauchieburn.

The nicht before the bluidy fray,
  Doon i' the birken lair
She got her Jamie's partin' kiss,
  An' a love lock o' his hair.
O Jeanie greet na thus for me,
  My battle graith is good,
I dinna dree the comin' fecht
  For mony a ane I've stood.
Thus Jamie spak to comfort her
  As to his neck clung she,
An' greetin' cried " O, Jamie dear,
  I fear me sair for thee."

But quickly frae her arms he gaed
  An' left the birken lair,
An' gaily shone his siller spurs
  All in the moonlicht fair.
Hame to her bower did Jeanie gang,
  An' laid her on her bed,
· Wi' Jamie's lock o' bonnie hair
  Beneath her dowie head.
An' lyin' there she dreamed she saw
  The spurs her Jamie wore,
But rusted was their siller sheen
  An' dabbled o'er wi' gore,—
She heard the shouts o' warlike men
  In battle's grim array,
An' saw her lover's sable steed
  Rush reinless 'mid the fray.

          .   .   .   .   .

The mornin' sun rose bricht an' fair
  That shone on Sauchieburn,
But saw, ere settin', mony a wife
  An' mony a maiden mourn.
Richt valiant did the loyal knights
  For Scotland's fated King

That day against the rebel host
  Their fiery chargers fling,
Fu' oft against the fatal spears
  That knightly tide came on,
An' foremost o' the chargin' host
  Young Jamie's armour shone.
Richt downward on the towering spears
  Again brave Jamie bore,
But ere the shock the siller spurs
  Were dabbled o'er wi' gore.

A cloth yard arrow swift an' keen,
  Sped by an archer true,
Struck down young Jamie in its flight
  An' pierced his body through.
Thus died as brave a knight as e'er
  Did death or danger spurn,
A sample of the gallant Scots
  That fell at Sauchieburn.
Noo reinless rushed the sable steed
  Across the gory plain,
While Jamie in his armour bricht
  Lay stretched amang the slain.
When gloamin' fell fair Jeanie hied
  Down to the birken lair,
But O! her heart was sair distressed,
  For Jamie wasna there.

Yestreen he promised ere he gaed
  To meet me here again,
An' blythely prove that a' my fears
  For him had been in vain.
O sair I fear yon vision's true
  Last nicht I saw sae grim,
My love will never come to me
  But I will gang to him.
An' wailin' thus wi' bitter moan

Fair Jeanie's footsteps turn
In sorrow frae the birken lair
  To bloody Sauchieburn.
An' by the pale moonlicht that shone
  Upon the silent dead,
She found her Jamie's manly form
  Stretched on its gory bed.

Neist morn the warders stout an' stern
  O' Elden Thristle Ha'
There found on Sauchieburn field
  The faithful lovers twa ;
An' stark in death by Jamie's side
  Young Jeanie lay fu' fair,
An' baith lie buried in one grave
  Down by the birken lair.

𝔅annockburn.

JUNE'S sun upon that summer morn
  Rose o'er our Northern land,
  And saw the haughty Southron hosts
  In battle order stand.
Their swords in thousands flashing bright,
  In·serried ranks their spears,
Might well have filled yon patriot band
  With anxious doubts and fears.
But He who nerves the patriot's heart
  And gives his arm the power
To smite oppression's armies down
  Was with them in that hour.

The men of Scotland knelt to pray,
  The Lord of Hosts did hear ;

The scoffing Saxons mock the sight,
    But in their hearts is fear.
Yet on they come with martial tread
    And banners streaming fair,
While loud their battle shouts resound
    And fill the troubled air.
The king of Scotland marks that wave
    Of tyranny advance,
While proudly o'er it as it rolls
    Gay plumes and pennons dance.

And turning to his trusty band
    That stand in firm array,
Cries " Men of Scotland, freedom lives
    Or dies with us this day."
An answering shout to heaven arose,
    All Albyn's hills resound ;
The Southron legions quail with dread
    Before that awful sound.
As forests sway before the blasts
    That o'er the mountains wheel,
So 'fore the hardy Scottish host
    Their dense battalions reel.

The Caledonians fiercely ply
    The battle-axe and spear,
And through the Saxon helmets fast
    The flashing claymores shear.
With gallant Randolph at their head
    The horsemen as of yore
Charged through the Southron bowmen bold
    And smote them to the core.
As lies the corn on harvest fields
    Behind the reapers' blade,
Or forest leaves when Autumn's past,
    So lay the English dead.

Their plumes and banners, rent and torn,
  Lay mingled with the slain,
While far and wide the fatal field
  Was drenched with crimson rain.
The morning sun beheld the might
  Of England's pomp and pride,.
Her gleaming columns stretching far
  Like silver-crested tide;
The setting sun his parting beams
  Threw o'er a bloody field,
Strewn with the reeking carnage red,
  The broken spear and shield.

And flying fast the vanquished hosts
  All broken and dismayed,
So late that stood in martial pride
  For battle fierce arrayed.
Now on that field stands mighty Bruce,
  And round him Scotland's brave,
While 'mid them o'er the streaming turf
  The Lion flag doth wave,
Its folds are dyed of crimson hue
  In England's dearest tide,
For round it fell 'neath patriot arms
  The flower of England's pride.

That glorious boon our fathers won
  On Bannockburn's plain,
O ! blessed freedom we their sons
  For ever shall maintain,
And to our children leave the gift
  Of freedom and our fame
All unimpaired, and trust that they
  May keep old Scotland's name.

—◇—

Charge of the Light Brigade.

THE bugles shrilly sound advance!
 In air six hundred sabres glance,
 And fierce six hundred chargers prance—
  They smell the fray afar.
Their nostrils quiver in their pride,
For heroes in their saddles ride
Whose fame shall ring the world wide
  While memory endures.

Like flash of light to join the fight
They swiftly pass before the sight,
Unbroken in their pride and might,
  As waves of ocean roll.
Both France and Britain's deep amaze
Is on their faces as they gaze
All powerless now to stop the pace
  To death that bears them on.

Around them, as they onward dash,
On every side grim cannons flash,
And rend the air at every crash
  With death in leaden showers.
Each warrior's heart with ardour glows,
As fast the ghastly gaps they close,
But faster still the bullet mows
  That gallant squadron down,

But now they're on the hated foe,
Now falls the long suspended blow,
And swift as arow from a bow
  They pierce the Russian line.
Down go the foe on every side,
And Britain's steel, all crimson dyed,
Reeks with the dripping gory tide
  As Moscow's columns reel.

Then back their desperate way they hew
In close array, like Britons true,
And loud they cheer the gallant few
 Who're left of all the band.
Ho! live for aye in song ye brave,
And flowers immortal deck your grave,
And brightest 'mong our laurels wave
 The wreath that tells your fame.

—◇—

The Huntly Soldier.

A SOLDIER of the Ninety-third, his tartans dyed
 with gore,
 Lay 'mong his wounded comrades amid the
 battle's roar,
While overhead the Indian sun a fiery globe did
 blaze,
And water! water! was the cry each parched throat
 did raise.
The pibroch of the Highlanders was sounding fierce
 and free,
And far amid the ranks of war their bayonets he could
 see,
As on they swept to victory, then heaved his breast
 with pride,
For men were there from Huntly upon sweet Deveronside.

And leaning on his knapsack, then he felt with bitter
 pain
That he might die, and never see his home and friends
 again;
Oh! could he but his parents see and one sweet
 maiden fair,
E

He would die at peace, contented a soldier's grave to
 share.
The tide of life was ebbing fast, and there upon the
 sand
He lay, while through the haze of death he saw his
 native land ;
Uprose his fevered fancy, and o'er the ocean wide
It bore him back to Huntly upon sweet Deveronside.

He thought 'twas evening, and he heard his aged
 parents pray
To God to watch their darling son 'mid dangers far
 away,
And bring him safe to them again unhurt as on that
 morn
He left them, soldier-hearted, and laughed their fears
 to scorn.
And one sweet maiden fair he saw, and clasped her
 in his arms,
And drank again the blissful tide of Love's endearing
 charms,
And saw her smile as when he said, "I'll make you
 my dear bride
When I come back to Huntly upon sweet Deveronside."

But never more did he return, for ere the close of day
His lifeless body 'mid the ranks of dead and wounded
 lay ;
His face was turned to Scotland, and each bleeding
 comrade near
Was thinking of that distant land to all their hearts
 so dear.
By morning light the Ninety-third had dug their
 soldiers' grave,
And in one deep and yawning trench they laid their
 kilted brave ;

And 'mong the martial sleepers there in foreign grave
  so wide,
Lies one that came from Huntly upon sweet Deveronside.

———◇———

Burns' Anniversary.
JAN. 25TH, 1882.

ONE hundred years and twenty three
    Expire upon this morn,
  Since he the soul of poetry
  To deathless fame was born,—
    As meteor gleams athwart the night
    He burst on men with glorious light—
    A spirit half divine.

Undying bard, the rolling years
    Add lustre to thy name,
And each succeeding race reveres
    Thy génius and thy fame.
    While history and tradition breathe,
    O! fadeless green shall be the wreath
    Of Scotland's Robert Burns.

The grandest measures of his lyre
    For love and freedom rise,
And wake in every breast the fire
    That inward smouldering lies.
    My glowing soul control doth spurn,
    And leaps to read his "Bannockburn,"
    Great ode of liberty.

That spirit-thrilling martial lay
    Paints Scotland's darkest hour,

When tyrant's chains nigh barred her way
    To freedom's glorious power;
        But mark, the hardy patriot band
        That followed Wallace take their stand
            To conquer or to die.

I see their fiercely flashing blades
    Glint in the sunlight fair,
I see their waving ancient plaids
    And broad blue bonnets there,
        And heavenward swelling clear and high
        I hear their one united cry
            Of liberty or death !

In Scotia's lowly homes at night,
    When glows the hearth-fire warm,
The toil-worn peasant's heart grows light
    Touched by our poet's charm,
        And bounds anew with relish rare
        Of "Tam o' Shanter" and his scare
            That wo'ful market night.

The "cottar" home imbues his mind
    With reverence and awe;
Its noble lesson helps to bind
    Him closer to that law,
        Which makes a people truly great
        And ornaments a home or State
            Far more than regal show.

The art to paint the flowers of earth
    Immortal bard was thine;
The tear of woe and smile of mirth
    Attend thy varying line.
        And humble virtue's fairest white
        Seems shimmered with a purer light
            O'er-haloed by thy song.

No palace echoed to thy tread,
  But genius on thy brow
Did coronet the noble head
  That but to God did bow.
    And evening winds by banks of Ayr
    Oft bore aloft the whispered prayer
    That breathed of love to all.

Our youths and maidens fondly pore
  Rapt o'er thy page with sighs,
And feels the thrill that moves the core
  When first affections rise ;
    And in their hearts for ever green
    Shall live each tender witching scene
    Thy magic songs reveal.

In every clime beneath the sun
  Their strains are known and sung,
And human hearts been touched and won
  Where'er their notes have rung,
    They cheer the soldier at his post,
    And soothe the sailor tempest toss't
    Far on the bounding wave.

The rustic daisy's simple bloom
  Seems fresher to us now,
And brighter seems the yellow broom
  On every hill and knowe,
    And clearer flow our streams along,
    Because the " ploughman poet's " song
    Reflects their beauties all.

One hundred years and twenty three
  Expire upon this morn,
And yet his soul of poetry
  Seems only newly born.

As meteor gleams athwart the night
He burst on men with glorious light,
But with no transient glow.

When Scotia's thistle dies and droops
Upon its native soil,
Or when an honest Scotsman stoops
To shrink from honest toil,
Then shall the soul of Burns flee
And chains instead of liberty
Be our ignoble doom.

The Smiddy.

O the smiddy last nicht, awa' doon by the craig,
I gaed to get fasten't a shoe on my naig,
An' to hear a' the uncos an' stories sae rare,
For the maist o' the news o' the country is there.
There's Brookie, the smith, wi' his snuff-mull in han',
Relatin'—for troth he's a wonderfu' man—
Some weel-foundit facts o' his ain observation
That lately he's studiet on "Man's Derivation,"
Forby his relations to hell an' the deevil,
An' proneness to imitate everything evil;
Hoo Popery's increasin', and warlike intentions
Pervade a' thae meetin's ca'd peacefu' conventions.
Then lang Tam, the darger, he's famed far an' near
For wonderfu' tales (he's a wonderfu' leer),
Tak's his pipe frae his cheek and begins an oration
'Bout poachin' adventures wad beat the creation.
Ae nicht by the craigie he set a few snares,
Intendin' some big game to catch unawares,
An' when it got win' that Tam took a big boar
The country side roun' was set a' in a roar.
It chanced that a grumphic o' masculine gender,

When howkin' for herbs baith tastie an' tender,
Had wandert frae hame awa' doon by the craigie,
An' ane o' Tam's traps had closed on its leggie.
But Tam stoutly swore he had ta'en a wild boar,
An' tell't the same story to folks o'er an' o'er;
An' his look to the story sic terrors did len',
That each hair on oor heads stude strach upon en'.
An' then there was Geordie, the farmer o' Horn,
Sae skilled in the value o' cattle an' corn;
He commentit at len'th on the shorthorn breed,
An' the way in partic'lar sic cattle to feed.
He spak' o' the oilcakes an' meals to be had,
And said that sic trash was weel ken't to be bad;
He never had used them sin' he had a farm,
An' nae stock in the country sae free was o' harm.
They sat thus an' spak' thus aroun' the big fire,
An' o' stories an' sangs they seemed never to tire,
Or read frae the *Journal* the news o' the week,
Nae further for knowledge did thae worthies seek.
An' yet o' maist subjects they something aye ken,
An' mair o' their business than mony a ane
Wha struts empty-headed in grandeur sae gay,
An' thinks he is made o' a far finer clay.
Though humble their sphere they are noble in heart,
An' play in the drama o' life a true part;
Still happy wi' health in contentment they live,
An' though scanty their store they aye cheerfully give.

—◇—

The Heights of Alma.

HIGH on the Alma's frowning heights the crested
eagles shine
Above the dark and serried hosts of Russia's
battle line,

Where deadly cannon yawning wait, and bayonets
  fiercely gleam
To mow the brave and gallant ranks that dare to
  cross the stream.
Ho ! lift our British banners now, unroll each noble
  fold
And let the fields where they have waved in glory be
  retold,
'Twill rouse our martial British hearts, for ere this
  day be done
Those rugged heights, and swelling slopes, and
  batteries must be won.
Our bayonets bright ere fall of night shall drip with
  Russian gore,
And tame their crested eagle's pride and still their
  cannon's roar,
So mind the days when brave Sir Ralph 'neath
  Egypt's burning sun,
To combat led the British hosts and glorious victories
  won ;
Come tell our gallant soldiers young the hundred
  fields of Spain,
O'er which their colours proudly waved 'mid war's
  destructive rain ;
Tell them again those fields of death o'er which their
  flags were borne
Till every fold by hissing shot, to shreds was rent
  and torn.
Hark ! now the thunderous cannons loud are flashing
  fire and lead
To stay the passage of the brave that Alma's torrents
  wade,
Its glassy bosom, once so smooth, is foamy now and
  white
As thousands wildly breast its tide with eager manhood's might ;

And rending shot its waters plough with many a
deadly splash,
And bursting shells fly overhead with loud resonant
crash ;
But forward press our gallant men with hearts as
true and bold
As those that won our laurel wreaths on bloody fields
of old.
I hear above the combat dread Old England's mighty
cheer
Triumphantly ring o'er the ranks from noble front
to rear,
And fierce and wild far up the heights brave Scotland's war pipes shrill—
Her kilted sons to victory lead upon that desperate
hill.
And mingling with the English cheer and Scotland's
battle cry,
True Irish hearts send up the shout "Old Erin do or
die."
And side by side, 'mid fire and blood, as on our fields
of yore,
They tamed the Russian eagle's pride and stilled
their cannon's roar ;
They stemm'd the rolling Alma's tide, and so on their
bayonets bright
In victory flashed along the crest of all the death
swept height,
And Britain's grand old battle flag, that many a field
has braved,
O'er Alma's bloody heights at last in triumph proudly
waved.

—◇—

Holyrood.

THE pibroch that through Holyrood, in days of
    "Auld Lang Syne,"
    Once poured its strains to courtly dance of lords
        and ladies fine,
Resounds no more through Holyrood, departed is the
    day
Its martial music filled those halls of Scottish pomp
    so gay.

Departed are the ancient times of Scotland's sceptred
    might,
No longer Kings of Scotland lead their vassals to the
    fight;
No longer do the plaided clans from Highland glens
    afar
Pour down in streams of Celtic fire, to join the ranks
    of war.

Where is our ancient glory now--where is our ancient
    fame ?
Our sires, if they uprose, would seek again their
    graves in shame,
To think the laurels that they won on many a hard-
    fought field
Are now transferred by us, their sons, to blazon Eng-
    land's shield.

Let them that think 'tis better so, think tamely on,
    say I,
But where's the patriot can behold Dunedin's Castle*
    high,
And look upon the jewelled crown that circled Bruce's
    head,

*Dunedin—The ancient name for Edinburgh.

And heave no sigh for days of yore, and Scottish
  glory fled.
Brave Scottish hearts in distant lands prove still that
  Scotland's name
Can never die, nor her renown dishonour know or
  shame;
Where'er our now united flags in danger are un-
  furled,
A Scot can still prove Scotland's might o'er all the
  vaunted world.

But never let a Scot pass by Dunedin's Castle bold,
And gaze upon that sacred rim of ancient Scottish
  gold—
The mighty sword and sceptre, too, there in repose
  that lie,
And heave not for old Scotland's sake a patriotic
  sigh.

For now no more in Holyrood, 'mong lords and ladies
  fine,
The pibroch's note is heard, as in the days of " Auld
  Lang Syne;"
Those noble halls in days of yore with regal pomp
  that shone,
Deserted are and silent now—with all their glory
  gone.

The Ploughman's Evening.

'TIS six by the clock, an' the sun in the west
    Tells ploughmen it's time for unyokin' an' rest,
  To hie to their supper, though humble the board,
The food that made Scotland aye on it is stored.

The brose an' the porridge there's naething can beat—
They're halesome, they're hardy, they're tastie an'
    sweet ;
They were food to our fathers, to Wallace an' Bruce,
The heroes wha conquered the English sae crouse.

Sae stick to the porridge, the brose, an' the kail,
An' for men o' guid muscle we never will fail ;
Still " Scotland for ever," oor war cry an' cheer,
Will frighten a' foemen wha venture us near.

The supper noo finished, the fire they sit roon
To hear frae the foreman the news o' the toon,
Where he'd been wi' his horses disposin' o' corn,
An' tastin' forby they could see o' the horn.

He spak' at sic random, the spittle it flew
'Tween the whiffs o's pipe in a stream frae's moo' ;
An' swore at some engine he'd met on the road,
For's horses nigh bolted an' coupet their load.

Noo just at this crisis, frae some neebor farm
Some laddies drap in, an' ye'll think it nae harm,
To kittle the lasses an' hear a bit sang,
The evenings when lanesome are eerie an' lang.

Or maybe some callant the fiddle can trim,
Inspirin' wi' music a shak' o' a lim' ;
Sae on to the floor in a jiffey they bounce,
An' wildly in " foursomes " they caper an' flounce.

At toeing Strathspeys, or at dancin' the " fling,"
The ploughman's the lad that a' ithers can ding ;
An' as for the lasses, sae blithesome an' braw,
A' your high born dames to them's naething ava.

O ! weel may auld Scotland be prood o' her queans
Sae strappin' an' bonnie when they're in their teens !

An' to match wi' her lads the world has but few—
Napoleon confess'd this at red Waterloo.

The lads wi' the tartan did never yet cower
When placed in the thick o' the fierce leaden shower;
An' the "Greys," when they charge in gallant array,
Decide in a twinklin' the fate o' the day.

The maist o' these chiels did the horses ance ca'
Till the blast o' the bugle beguiled them awa';
An' at times in the markets you'll see them again
Recruitin' sae dandy wi' gloves an' a cane.

Or owre a bit gill in the "Black Bull" maybe
Wi' cronies o' yore they'll be a' in their glee,
Recalli· ¯ auld stories an' pranks to the min'
O' their ploughboy life in the days o' "lang syne."

—◇—

The Scot Abroad.

HOW strange 'mid a' the care an' strife,
      An' varying ups an' doons o' life,
   Nae matter where you chance to roam,
   You'll find a Scot has made his home.
He suits the mountain or the plains,
Alike the scorching heats an' rains;
Though foreign climes hae bronzed his skin,
His heart remains unchanged within.
He deigns to ape nae foreign styles,
Or learn their trickster foreign wiles,
But plays an honest Scotchman's part,
Wi' skilfu' han' an' manly heart.
He gets respect where'er he goes,
Frae Scotland's frien's or Scotland's foes,

An' where the weak's oppress'd by micht
He'll use his power to set them richt.
Just like his nation's emblem grand—
The thistle o' his native land—
Wha him assails wi' blustering brag
Will get indeed a wofu' jag.
But brither Scots, just see them meet,
An' a' adjourn their throats to weet
Oot ower the days o' " Auld Lang Syne,"
I trow it is a sicht divine.
There roarin' mirth aye croons the board,
An' Scotland yet's " the drinking word ;
An' pledged it is wi' three times three,
In reamin' stoups o' " barley bree."
Ye foreign loons ye well may stare,
If you should chance to see them there,
Their rugged features smoothed away
Ower tales o' home an' youth's bright day.
The waving woods o' shaggy broon,
An' mountain torrents foamin' doon,
They see in memory's e'e sae clear,
Through mony a lang an' weary year,
The gowden whins an' gowany lea,
The yellow corn an' reapers free ;
A' these come back wi' tenfold power
To croon wi' joy this social hour.
Their cherished hope's to cross the main,
To dear auld Scotia back again,
An' spend amid their native braes
Wi' dearest frien's their closing days.

Eviction.

A Protest against the Depopulation of the Highlands, and the Substitution of Deer Forests for Human Dwellings.

WHY should honest men be hunted
From the land that gave them birth,
Making room for game to flourish
In their place upon the earth?

Why should aged sires and mothers,
With their children at their knee,
Thus be driven forth as felons
From a land that's boasted free?

All to foster proud ambition
Are those lowly sons of toil
Driven from their lowly dwellings—
Tyranny usurps the soil.

Surely God who made the peasant
Meant him not to houseless roam,
Nor empower'd a lordly mortal
Thus to waste his lowly home.

Famed were Britain's peasant soldiers
In the past and noble days,
When her ranks were filled with thousands
Fresh from Scotia's heathy braes.

By the hearths where grew those heroes
Now the red deer grazes free,
But the men are gone for ever,
And their race no more we'll see.

Britain, in the hour of danger,
Where will be thy peasant shield?
Where the arms that drove thy bayonets,
Hearts that knew not how to yield?

In that hour when help is needed
  Will the lordlings of the land,
With their game preserves and forests,
  Prove a strong defensive band?

Spain hath seen proud Gallic armies
  Tremble at the ringing cheer
Of our gallant Highland soldiers;
  Will they tremble at our deer?

Lords there are who earn the title
  By their dignity and worth;
Men who gain their meed of honour
  For themselves and not their birth.

Men who bravely aid and labour,
  Striving for the common good,
And who scorn in heart to mingle
  With the lazy gilded brood.

Patriots they of manly virtue,
  Nature's nobles to the core;
May our country, to its credit,
  Nurse and cherish many more.

Let us fill the glens and forests
  Once again with sturdy men;
Better sight than sportmen's rifles
  Are the mowers 'mong the grain.

Bring us back those men, they're wanted
  In this nineteenth century time;
Men of mind and men of muscle,
  Fit to live in any clime.

Men who feel and know they're equal
  To the sterner tasks of life;
Ever ready, brave, and willing
  For the ceaseless human strife.

Men of bold and dauntless bearing,
　And who care not for the frown
Of an irate, brainless lordling,
　Angry 'cause his day has flown.

Yes, the day is past forever,
　When at scowl of titled fools
Honest poverty shall tremble—
　Ours is lore of later schools.

Honour men not for their station,
　Nor their silver, nor their gold ;
Honest worth in manly bosoms
　Is not bartered, bought, or sold.

Gift it is from mighty Donor,
　Maker of both high and low ;
Rank and title are but bubbles,
　Rising as life's waters flow.

Strain not after airy visions
　That may float around thee gay ;
Eager chase they, but evade it,
　Or in grasping fade away.

Study how to help a brother,
　How to cheer a fellow-man ;
Aim at good that's universal,
　Help to make all peoples one.

Yours may then be honours brighter
　Than are won by shield and sword ;
Yours a name of fame forever,
　Living, lasting, and adored.

* Porter Fair.

THE term time wi' merry May
   Has come again ance mair,
An' a' the lads an' lasses gay
   Are gaun to Porter Fair.

Frae a' the roads they're troopin' in,
   In jovial crowds sae rare ;
The country lad is far ahin'
   That's nae at Porter Fair.

The ploughman loon, sae brisk an' braw,
   This day is free o' care ;
He'll see his merry cronies a'
   Again at Porter Fair.

It's nae sae aft he has a day,
   An' ready cash to spare ;
Nae wonder that his spirit's gay
   Wi' thochts o' Porter Fair.

The sweetie stan's alang the streets
   Display their temptin' ware ;
An' mony ither grander treats
   Are seen at Porter Fair.

The country laddies hug an' kiss
   Their sonzie lasses there,
An' ither things that are amiss
   They dae at Porter Fair.

In crowded inns, the "barley bree"
   Gies wings to a' his care—
The ploughman's fairly on the spree
   This day at Porter Fair.

* Turriff feeing market.

Blin' fiddlers scrape wi' a' their micht
   The cat-gut an' the hair,
To dancers reelin' wrang an' richt,
   Iu crowds at Porter Fair.

An' warblers o' the tinker train,
   Wi' lungs o' vigour rare,
Sing deeds of old in warlike strain
   To stir up Porter Fair.

They hoarsely shout o' mony a field
   O' battle teuch an' sair,
Where Scotland's foes aye backward reel'd,
   Though thick as Porter Fair.

The feein' too gaes briskly on
   Wi' burly farmers there ;
They ken he's aye a decent loon
   They fee at Porter Fair.

They ken he'll ploo' a bonnie rig,
   An' o' their horse tak' care ;
An' sae they fee him, clean an' trig,
   That day at Porter Fair.

The day noo ower, they hameward plod—
   The lads an' lasses fair,
An' troth it is a merry road
   That leads frae Porter Fair.

The lads half fou the lasses lo'e,
   An' for them ocht wad dare,
Ayo vowin' true, wi' mou' to mou',
   The nicht o' Porter Fair.

Nor will they part, they are sae fain,
   Ilk ardent loving pair,
Till dawn proclaims the day again
   That follows Porter Fair.

Peter o' Berbithill.

UPON the merry harvest field
  Nae man the scythe could better wield
    Than Peter o' Berbithill.
His sweepin' stroke could clear the rig,
An' keep a'body at a jig
    That followed him wi' will.

The hairsters that came in his wake,
Doon to the laddie at the rake,
    Aye laggit far ahin'.
They did their best ilk lass an' man,
An' wi' the sheaves the stookers ran
    Till a' were oot o' win'.

But a' in vain, still far afore
The glancin' scythe o' Peter tore,
    An' urged them to come on,
Till wet wi' sweat was ilka sark,
An' a' declared 'twas killin' wark
    Wi' mony a pech an' groan.

May Peter flourish on the braes,
An' peace an' plenty croon his days,
    An' bairnies roond him spring
To solace him in after years
When wearin' doon this vale o' tears,
    As maun a' livin' thing.

An' when he's auld he'll surely min'
On corn rigs o' Auld Langsyne,
    When he could beat them a';
Ae day wi' him upon the field
Made boastin' chaps the palm to yield,
    An' stop their brag an' blaw.

But scythin' days are nearly run,
Wi' a' the store o' mirth an' fun
    That eased their labour sair ;
Noo great machines cut doon the corn,
An' scythes are cast aside wi' scorn
    To rust in disrepair.

—◇—

Johnny Pirrie.

YE jolly farmers o' the North,
    Around your ingles cheery,
        Come back me up to sing the worth
Of honest Johnny Pirrie.

Nae man there is, baith far and near,
    Through Banffshire braid and bonnie,
But what wid gie a rousin' cheer
    And hip hurrah ! for Johnny.

Ilk farmer billie kens him weel,
    Sae cantie aye an' merry ;
An' when a beast's in need o' skeel
    They rin for Johnny Pirrie.

When horse an' kye are like to dee
    Wi' troubles sair an' mony ;
Like win' their owners ye will see
    Aye tak' the road for Johnny.

A stirk may choke upon a neep,
    Or stick a coo in calvin',
An' a' the fouk be i' the greip
    About the beastie tauvin'.

But soon the stot will redd its throat,
   An' lowe baith hale an' bonnie ;
But faith it wasna worth a groat
   Without the aid o' Johnny.

An' soon the coo a calf will hae,
   As plump as ony cherry,
That wad hae been as dead's a strae
   But for auld Johnny Pirrie.

A deein' horse rou'd roon' wi' rugs,
   If ye but summon Johnny,
Will live to kick and cock its lugs,
   And niccar yet wi' ony.

By day an' nicht, in dark or licht,
   At hour an' minute ony,
Whate'er is wrang will be set richt,
   Gin ye but sen' for Johnny.

A heart made o' the sterling stuff—
   True grit frae Nature's quarry—
A helpin' han' an' muscle tough,
   Belong to Johnny Pirrie.

His han' ne'er took a hirelin's fee—
   His skill is free to ony ;
Sae wish ilk honest man wi' me
   Lang life an' health to Johnny.

—◇—

The Pibroch.

TRUE Scottish hearts with pride it thrills,
   That wild war music of the hills,
      From pibroch of the brave.

In martial measures loud and free
Its stirring song of liberty
    Might nerve the meanest slave.

The Scottish blood in all our veins
Fast courses as its magic strains
    Each heart with ardour fires ;
For in that rousing, ringing strain
Each patriot hears the voice again
    That led his gallant sires.

Thou'rt worthy of our meed of praise,
And honour to the latest days,
    Thou pipe of deathless fame ;
And at thy sound may hearts aye bound,
And noble Scottish men be found,
    To venerate thy name.

Oppression's chains can never bind
The hardy race of valiant mind
    That owns the pibroch grand—
Whose courage-breathing martial strain,
Has led on many a bloody plain
    Auld Scotia's warrior band.

How proudly 'mong our hills and dells
Triumphantly its music swells,
    And rings the glens along !
E'en mountain eagles, soaring high,
Swoop downward from their native sky,
    To catch the fearless song ;

And echo sends the chorus forth
Upon the wild winds of the north,
    Till every royal Ben*
Re-echoes back in measures free
That brave old song of liberty
    And pride of Scottish men.

*Our mountain Bens.

Muckle Geordie.

AT kirk an' fair a bonnet braid
 You'll see on Muckle Geordie's head;
In auld Kilmarnock it was made
   The year o' Waterloo,
An' has a monster tap o' red,
   This famous bonnet blue.
Within its ample folds sae tough
His pipe, tobacco, an' his snuff,
Wi' lots o' ither orra stuff,
   Are hidden frae the view,—
The bonnet hauds a bushel rough
   O' taties when its fou'.

The braidest bonnets e'er I saw
Compared wi' Geordie's were but sma';
For rain, an' hail, an' sleet, an' snaw
   Micht fa' in torrents roun',
His bonnet big defies them a'
   To wet his honest croon.
An' Geordie, like the maist o' men,
Has ae great hobby o' his ain,
An' kickin' horse an' mules to train
   Is his especial game,
An' then to sell them aff again
   Whene'er he has them tame.

Through trysts an' markets wi' a stride,
Goliath-like, sae slow an' wide,
He ranges, wi' a conscious pride,
   In quest o' vicious fare;
An' when a savage beast is spied
   He buys it then an' there;
An' loupin' on the beastie's back,
He gies its hide a rousin' whack
That echoes like a pistol crack

Among the thievin' craws,
For Geordie has a wondrous knack
O' layin' on the tawse. ·

Then wi' a loud triumphant shout
He wheels the naig to right about,
An' gallopin' through folk an' nowte,
　He tak's the road for hame,
Wi' twa'r-three jugs o' liquor stout
　A-splashin' in his wame.
O' canny Scots, sic samples noo,
Alas! are growin' unco few ;
The risin' race, wi' notions new,
　Hae changed the time o' day,
An' Geordie's class, wi' bonnets blue,
　Are wearin' fast away.

The Dying Fireman.

MY dearest frien's, around my bed I see you
　　waefu' stand,
　　An' watch wi' burstin' hearts the grains o' life's
　　fast-runnin' sand ;
I canna live, though fain I would, I see my settin'
　sun
Sink 'yond the western hills o' life ere half my day
　be done ;
It grieves me sair, I canna thole to see your hearts
　sae wrung,
The twilight gathers roun' me noo ; it's hard to dee
　sae young.

Farewell to earth an' a' its joys, frail life for me is
　done ;
Adieu! the gallant fire brigade, my comrades every
　one.

I might hae lived to manhood's prime but for that
    fatal stair ;
I leaped on it 'mid fire an' smoke, and blinded by the
    glare
I saw not that my weight was laid upon a blazing
    rung
That snapped an' threw me to the ground ; it's hard
    to dee sae young.

I might hae lived to manhood's prime, but why should
    I regret ?
Twa lives I saved, an' wad a third but for my hapless
    fate ;
I only did, wi' willing heart, what Duty bade me do ;
For every man in oor brigade is ready, staunch, and
    true,
An' leaps alert upon the car whene'er the bell is rung
That tells o' fire ; but ah ! my frien's, its hard to dee
    sae young.

There' One on high that kens my heart ; I'm waiting
    for His hand
To guide me through the shady vale to His ain pro-
    mised land.
Mair o' my thoughts He might hae got, but those He
    got were true,
An' I hae faith that in this hour He'll nae forsake
    me noo,
An' you, my aged mother dear, that o'er my cradle
    hung,
O! greet nae mair, I'm ready, though its hard to dee
    sae young.

I go, farewell ! my eyes are dim, Death's chilly hand
    I feel
Freeze up the life-blood o' my heart, an' o'er my senses
    steal.

My brow is cold, an' all is dark, the sting o' pain is
    gone —
A minute mair, an' I shall kneel before my Maker's
    throne,
An' join my voice unto the throng, an' hear His
    praises sung,
Who came to earth an' willing died for us when He
    was young.

The Wanderer's Return.

BEHOLD the wanderer's features, tanned
    In many a far and foreign land.
    Beam with the transport that he feels
    To tread once more his native strand,

To see the mountains, heather crowned,
    Glow in their wealth of purple bloom,
Or, swathed in mist, their summits rear,
    In naked grandeur and in gloom.

Or o'er the rocks the mountain streams
    In foam their currents wildly pour,
While through the woody glens resound
    The echoes of their sullen roar.

Emotion deep his bosom swells,
    His eye is dimmed by manly tears,
Again to view the scenes beloved
    'Mong which he spent his early years.

There stands the cot beside the wood,
    The same sweet brooklet running near,
It murmurs still the same old song
    That long ago he loved to hear.

Though scenes through which in life we range
  Were beauteous Nature's choicest bowers,
None bind the heart with lasting charm
  Like those which saw our youthful hours.

———◆———

The Harvest Home.

IT was the time when golden leaves
    Were mixing wi' the green,
  An' stubble fields showed where the sheaves
    Of corn had lately been ;
When sportsmen chiels, wi' dog an' gun,
    In quest o' game did roam,
  Ae nicht we did convene wi' fun
    To haud oor Harvest Home.

The lasses, bless the darlin's a',
    (To this you'll say Amen)
  To please the lads were buskit braw
    In dresses neat an' plain.
An' ilka lad wi' brush an' comb
    Had made himsel' fu' smart,
  Alike to grace the Harvest Home
    An' win some lassie's heart.

When Geordie smiles in Jennie's face,
    She blushes to the croon,
  An' thinks on mony a stowen kiss
    Beneath the harvest moon.
When leadin' late for fear o' rain,
    Somehow by hook or crook,
  He kissed her owre an' owre again
    At ilka ither stook—

All heedless o' the raiker loon,
　Whase ire they had awoke
By chasin' ane anither roon',
　An' scatterin' a' the "brock."
But a' the merry toil was by,
　An' noo in blythesome glee
Did sparkle every beamin' eye,
　An' every heart beat free.

On chairs an' deals they sit them roon'
　The ample table spread,
There at the en' the raiker loon,
　The maister at the head,
An' solemnly the grace he says,
　That crops may never fail,
But grow abundant a' the days
　That he on earth may dwell.

Then ilka ane a spoon taks up,
　Wi' appetite fu' hale,
To scramble for the ring, an' sup
　The glorious "meal an' ale."
An' he or she wha gets the ring
　May happy be indeed,
For, just as sure as onything,
　They'll married be wi' speed.

But surely fortune helps the brave
　At times to win the fair,
For Geordie soon among the lave
　Hauds up the emblem rare,
An' mid a ringin' loud hurrah!
　He swaggers to his feet,
An' gallantly the ring sae braw
　Presents his Jennie wi't.

Then comes the tea, the toast, an' fish,
　An' cakes o' crumpy bread,

As much an' mair's the heart could wish
   O' ony man or maid.
An' syne the muckle whisky pig—
   The maister brings it in,
An' ilka lad a glass maun swig
   To set his legs in bin ;

For twa guid fiddlers noo commence
   Their fiddles gran' to tune,
Which gars the lads begin to dance
   An' lasses whirl roon'.
The fiddlers noo are fairly richt,
   Baith playin' rare an' weel,
An' ilka ane wi' a' their micht
   Gaes tearin' through the reel.

Ho ! how they sped the floor aroou,
   Wi' caperin' an' swingin',
The very ceilin' creaked aboon
   Wi' din an' music ringin' ;
An' thus the merry hours flew by
   Wi' dancin' an' wi' jestin',
Dull sleep was far frae every eye,
   An' nae ane thocht o' restin'.

Auld Scotia's dances ane an' a'
   That nicht were trippit weel
By mony a merry lassie braw,
   An' mony a strappin' chiel.
An' when the mornin' stars grew faint
   In Heaven's distant dome
"Lang Syne" was sung, an' thus we en't
   Oor merry Harvest Home.

Faith and Reason.

BEHOLD meek Faith, with beaming eye,
Seek not to know or question why
This thing or that should be ;
But onward moving seek a goal
For her submissive, doubtless soul,
Meek-hearted, joyfully.

Faith looks beyond the roll of years,
And far beyond the starry spheres,
And sees a region bright,
Where, when she's past death's mystic gates,
Her glorious heritage awaits
'Neath skies of fadeless light.

She shrinks not at the dread abyss
Where doubt and error's waters hiss,
And shower their tainting spray ;
But, staff in hand, amid their roar,
And eye fixed on the further shore,
She calmly holds her way.

She murmurs not though hard the road,
And heavy be her thorny load,
Nor vents she sigh of pain ;
Serenely moves her patient form—
Amid the darkness and the storm,
The path to her is plain.

She sees amid the shades of time
A ray from Calvary's mount sublime
Light on her humble way ;
Its blessed light her bosom cheers,
And leads her through the " vale of tears "
Triumphant, safe, away.

But sceptic Reason views the tomb,
And says there's nought beyond the g oom
    His brilliant lamp can show ;
And groping vain in mortal might,
He scans, with torch of science bright,
    All things both high and low.

He sweeps the starry fields of air,
Unveiling all their glories rare
    To wondering mind and eye ;
But failing with his feeble light
To find the vaunted regions bright
    Beyond those spheres that lie,

He, mocking, asks where is the place
Of that celestial angel race,
    Of golden harps and song ?
I've scanned those distant airy globes
That each on high revolving throbs,
    But find no cherub throng.

Away ! ye phantoms of the brain,
With all dark superstition's train
    Of canting priests and prayer ;
Life's gospel is how best to thrive,
And pleasure drink while yet alive,
    Ere death with beasts we share.

Thus Faith and Reason onward go
Till life's faint taper flickers low,
    And both must cross the wave ;
'Tis then that craven Reason fails,
And wildly, lost, despairing wails,
    While humble Faith is brave.

Vision of Hell.

WHEN by the fire in Morpheus' arms
One night strange visions came in swarms,
All trooping through my wildered brain,
And last of all came Hell's domain.
An awful terror seized my soul
To hear the fiends incarnate howl
In carnival around the lost
Upon this burning sulphurous coast.
High on a dreadful throne of fire
The devil sat and tuned his lyre;
His demon fingers swept the chords
While danced around the hellish hordes.
In wild fantastic maze they reeled,
Anon they shrieked, and madly wheeled;
Their hair like fiery fibres gleamed,
And malice from their features beamed.
A scorching air was all around,
And writhing on the burning ground
In one vast mass, like shoals of worms,
Lay million hosts of human forms.
Their shrieks for mercy rose to heaven,
But time was past, and judgment given;
Their cries might well the earth have rent,
And made e en Satan's heart relent.
The rich and poor were mingled there,
From every clime of earth they were;
The black, the white, of every race,
Of every age, and every place.
There murderers red with human gore
In torments blasphemed still and swore;
And harsh oppressors there did lie
Who heard with scorn the helpless cry.
There lay hypocrisy unveiled
That here on earth 'gainst sin had railed,
With kings and sinners great and small.

G

From dens of vice, and regal hall.
The forests waved like fiery seas
Their glowing branches in the breeze
That scorching blew with sulphurous smell
O'er all the blazing fields of hell.
The streams which molten lava ran
Were bridged by many a flaming span ;
And burning meteors winged through space
With lightning speed their airy race.
In myriad hosts like rooks or crows
On wings the sable demons rose,
With horrid screams of feignèd woe
To mock the tortured mass below.
In eddying circles wild they flew,
And still their clamour louder grew ;
While fire tipped darts, red, stinging hot,
Like assegias below they shot.
Those grinning fiends, with eyes aglow,
Augmenting more the wrath and woe,
Kept up with frenzied glee the revels—
Congenial sport indeed to devils.
And "this is hell.   Oh! dread abyss,
A region of forsworn bliss "
I heard a demon loudly sing,
And dart at me with tiger spring.
I vented then a dreadful yell,
And woke as from my chair I fell,
And gasped aloud, nigh dead with fear—
" The Lord be praised, I still am here."
Now, sinners all who this may read,
Consider well the lives you lead,
And clamour loud at mercy's door
Ere yet the day of grace be o'er.
Could you but see that awful sight
Of direful woe I saw that night,
You'd quick forsake the path in time
That leads you to yon sultry clime.

An Evening Muse.

IN thoughtful mood as twilight fell
  One eve I sought a rustic dell
  To taste the sweets of Poesy's spell,
      And vent my Muse,
  And drink from out her mystic well
      Parnassian dews.

Far from the throbbing city's glare,
Its busy streets and murky air,
I felt the load of human care
      Take wings and fly
Away, away, I wist not where,
      Since far from I.

Here, hermit-like, from man apart,
I felt the life-blood through me dart
And tune the lyre-strings of my heart
      That late lay dumb,   .
And to the kindling strain impart
      Melodious hum.

Till soaring fancy spreads her wing,
Like lark that upward mounts to sing
And pipes until the cloudlands ring
      With quivering sound,
So fitful fancy, fervent thing,
      Soars starward bound.

The bardic soul attends her flight,
And peering looks in Time's vast night
Where dim expiring meteors light
      The murky maze,
And where beyond his farthest sight
      Stretch endless ways.

There, pillar'd in the night of time,
He sees weird structures rise sublime,
Whereon dim forms eternal chime
 Their endless lays,
And round whose forms uptowering clime
 Bright deathless bays.

Thus, fancy led, he seeks to rise
And skim the pure o'er-arching skies
To pluck a planet for his prize
 From out those tiers,
Whose blazing brilliance dims nor dies
 Throughout the years.

A thousand thousand years of night
Have darkened not their lustre bright,
And thousands more shall roll in flight
 Yet fail to dim
The glory of the stars that light
 The Cherubim.

O! feeble atom, mortal man,
Thy breath's but for a moment drawn
In that long day's eternal span
 We name Forever,
One hour of which thy proudest plan
 And work can shiver.

Thus musing doth the poet's soul
To fancy linked out-speed control,
And soaring o'er each bounding pole
 'Yond lines of earth,
Scan cloudy caves where thunders roll
 And storms have birth.

And gazing down where Libra's line
Celestial balance doth define,

Where in our night the sun doth shine
    With powerful ray,
He sees the gilded railroad twine
    That guides Sol's way.

Away to where the dog star's fire
In distance gleams like Grecian pyre
The raptured minstrel bears his lyre,
    And onward steers
As if to join the heavenly choir
    Whose song he hears.

Float thence from yonder seraph sphere,
Whose pearled gates he hovers near,
Within whose bounds no weary tear
    E'er dims the eyes,
Where sorrow's shade that haunts us here
    Can never rise.

There countless millions that have trod
Like us the bosom of this clod,
Returning spirit-robed to God,
    From whom they sprung,
Now scan life's weary mortal road
    With pilgrims throng.

And 'mid the pilgrim throng below
Bright guardian spirits unseen go,
Averting oft the stream of woe
    That surges round,
While demon forms flit to and fro
    On evil bound.

Deep skilled in every hellish wile
Those fiends lurk oft in luring smile
And subtle tongues of polished guile
    To lead astray,

Infesting every treacherous mile
　　Of life's highway.

Wrong and oppression, lust and war,
And slanderous words all demons are,
And ever raging near and far
　　They foully go
All human happiness to mar
　　And mix with woe.

Oh! that mankind would lend an ear
To voice of conscience when they hear
It whispering of some duty clear
　　Or noble plan,
Instead of nursing selfish fear
　　Of fellowman.

Then disappointment's venomed dart
Less frequently would gall the heart,
And life would be a joyous mart
　　With dealer's throng,
Where worthy deeds as wares would thwart
　　Exchange of wrong.

Then would the poor and helpless know
Less hardship, misery, and woe,
For men would seeds of kindness sow
　　And reap again,
When He, the Lord of high and low,
　　Binds up His grain.

—◇—

Lines to Erring Sisters.

ALL ye from virtue's fold who stray
　　To walk in shame and folly's way,

'Mong painted waifs in clothing gay
    And wreathed in smiles deceitful,
List to my song, if conscience lives,
And to your heart one impulse gives,
Think of the home mayhap that grieves
    Thy sinful wayward wandering;
And if no home for you doth mourn,
No friends to chide and none to spurn,
Oh! chide yourselves and timely turn—
    Fair virtue's fold awaits you.
See right ahead your direful doom
The darksome, loathsome harlot's tomb
Awaiting with its awful gloom
    To shroud your blighted bodies.
And ah! your souls once pure and fair,
Which die not, cannot enter there,
They live for aye; yes live—but where?
    Let now mute conscience answer.

And thou, too, man, who hast beguiled
Some stainless one and her defiled,
Then cast her off and sneering smiled
    To see her bowed in sorrow,—
Think not the deed has passed unseen,
And none shall reckon you between;
Soon shall th' avenging arrow keen
    Thy guilty bosom harrow.
Take heed, and in thy youth's bright day
Tread thou where virtue holds the sway,
And gilded paths, which lure away
    From rectitude, eschew them.
The paths of innocence seem bare,
No tempting flowers conceal a snare,
But happiness and peace are there
    With crowns of life immortal.

Modesty.

O! gentle modesty, thy winning way
All powerful is the hearts of men to sway,
Thou art indeed true woman's heavenly prize,
When stripped of thee her angel nature dies.
What is she then? a thing for us to scorn,
A beauteous blossom turned venomed thorn;
Shun, shun, oh! shun her all who bliss would know,
Nor mar your lives with bitterness and woe.

'Tis sweet to see a gentle maiden smile,
And hear her voice with tenderness beguile;
But mark the change when modesty hath flown,
And tones once gentle have assertive grown.
She for our solace and companion sent,
'Fore God and man her charter she hath rent;
How could we love, the heart recoils in dread,
And love's sweet place sad pity takes instead.

Yes, pity wrings the manly heart with pain
To see frail woman heaven's law disdain,
And stand usurper of the sterner place
For men appointed in the earthly race.
Sweet modesty, return on angel wing,
And render woman a thrice precious thing,
All worthy of our love and kindest care—
A gem of loveliness, a treasure rare.

—◇—

Love.

IN life's philosophy is there to tell
    What power is that which rivets by its spell,—
    That mystic spark, undying from above,
Men feel but see not, and they call it Love.

Speak love and tell us, for we grope in vain
With mortal hands to grasp thy magic chain
Whose subtle links have bound the soul of man
To kindred soul since human life began.
We wander aimless to a dreary goal
Till love alights its beacon in our soul,
Then life seems stripped of weariness and woe,
And earth shines fairer 'neath its kindly glow.
All things are brighter, and the flowerets fair
Breathe sweeter odours on a purer air ;
The warbler's song finds echo in our hearts,
And nature's smile a deeper joy imparts.
And in thy train comes charity, O ! love,
That sacred pilot to the realms above,
And 'neath thy touch our finite minds expand
And catch bright glimpses of the angel land.
Love ! boundless spirit from thy nectar'd lip
Ecstatic elexirs of bliss we sip ;
Thy whispered breathings like a cherub's sigh
Stir thoughts divine and aspirations high ;
Hearts bend in meekness to thy common law,
And from thy fount refining waters flow
Which nourish sentiments of noble worth
And purge our natures which are vile by birth.
Spread wide thy wings, O ! love, upon the land,
And touch all bosoms with thy magic wand,
Till spotless virtue and her virgin train
With thee in unity of bliss shall reign.

—◆—

Woman's Kiss.

N Eden's groves the powers above
Did sweets celestial pour,

Until the cup of human bliss
　　With nectar bubbled o'er.
Young love was Queen of Paradise
　　In these, life's early hours,
And soft and low the gentle winds
　　Breathed 'mong its virgin flowers.
An angel watched the happy pair
　　All primal blisses sip,
And saw that Adam relished most
　　The taste of Eve's sweet lip.
And when they sinned, and righteous Heaven
　　Upset the cup of bliss,
This angel saved one drop for man—
　　It was a woman's kiss.
And pleasure pure the Seraph felt,
　　As after races grew,
To note how man his drop of joy
　　Still from this fountain drew.
So more, to make the bliss complete,
　　He filled each maiden's breast
With fond desire for noble man
　　Her lips to freely taste.
Then, maidens, be not loth to give,
　　Nor, men, be slow to take,
When thus an angel deigned to save
　　The pleasure for your sake.

———◇———

The Sisters Three.

E foreign bards across the deep,
　　Unstring your harps and lowly weep;
　　No more their chords enraptured sweep
　　　　To praise your maidens fair.

For in our land doth beauty smile,
And deck the daughters of our isle
With every charm that can beguile
The heart of mortal man.

I know three seraph sisters young,
As fair as ever minstrel sung,
Or ever lover's bosom wrung,
With beauty's witching smile.

Sweet modesty adorns each face,
And crowns them queens among their race,
While round their light elastic pace
A subtle grace doth play.

Seek not amid Italian flowers
For maidens sweet in sunny bowers,
Where free the grape its juice out-pours,
And endless summer smiles.

Think not in climes beyond the sea,
Renowned for love and chivalry,
That beauty reigns in majesty,
And doth no rival know.

'Mid Caledonia's heathy hills,
And by her pure and sparkling rills,
Whose ceaseless music ever fills
The glens with melody,

The lights of love far brighter dance,
In every bonnie lassie's glance,
But o'er these all the smiles entrance
Of those sweet sisters three.

To Nameless Bards.

MY brethren of the tuneful throng,
   Unknown to fame we pour our song
     In measures wild and free,
With none to hear it but some friend
Who may their kind attention lend,
     Or laud our melody.
Yet eagerly we ply the quill,
And try to scale Parnassus' hill
     To win ourselves a name,
And from its envied heights to send
Our voices to the world's end
     In ringing notes of fame.
But nameless yet, and fameless yet,
Low at its base unseen we sit,
     And forth our music pour ;
While great and small go trooping by,
Nor deign on us to cast an eye—
     Our presence they ignore.
Despair ye not, ye nameless throng,
Who chant unheard your prompted song,
     Take courage, and be brave ;
Still lure the muse by every ruse,
And pour your ink in streams profuse—
     A sable bardic wave.
Resume the quill with dauntless will,
And try once more the rugged hill
     Where sit the " tuneful nine ; "
Then in their presence touch the lyre,
And pour your raptured songs of fire
     In numbers all divine ;
And ever let your noble strain
Be raised to banish gloom and pain ;
     From hearts that weary be ;
And mortals groping in the mire,

Teach them to think, and thus aspire
　　To knowledge—wisdom's key ;
Till man to man a brother prove,
And earth an Eden be of love
　　And grand fraternity—
Till states and peoples hand in hand
In harmony together stand,
　　And drink felicity.

—◇—

The Poet's Dream.

IN my early boyhood's day,
　　When the world seemed fair and gay,
When of dreams my heart was full,
Ere my head knew Wisdom's rule—
In that early happy time,
When my pen began to rhyme,
Said I to self—" I'll be a Poet,
Though the world may never know it.
I will write and wake the fire
Slumbering in my hidden lyre.
I will climb the famed Parnassus,
Whence I'll thunder to the masses
In a voice so full and strong
That 'twill draw the wondering throng ;
I will teach them to forget
All the irony of Fate,
To be happy and content
In the work to which they're sent,
Striving to be true and brave,
For their end is not the grave ;
Moving onward to that time
When the hearts of every clime
All shall beat about one throne
In a friendly unison,

When one universal rule
In the World's common school
Shall cement the Nations' souls,
From the Equator to the Poles.
Then the song-bird's carol shrill,
By each babbling silver rill
In the greening groves of spring,
Echo will a sweeter ring,
Full of joyous mirth and glee,
Simple, heart-felt melody ;
Waking many a gladsome thought
In all hearts with pleasure fraught,
While with trump and flag unfurled
Peace, as Empress of the world,
Shall proclaim her reign benign,
Crowned with laurel, and with vine;
Crushing strife's envenomed brood,
Making one great brotherhood,
Singing over land and sea—
One God, one law, and liberty
To Earth and all Humanity."

Such my dream, my dream sublime,
In my early boyhood's time,
And, although no mighty poet,
I would have the world know it,
That I see afar the gleam
Of the dawning of my dream.
Courage, brothers, you are one
In the Parliament of Man ;
Bravely act, feel not alone,
Help the groaning world on.

The Thames.

A THOUSAND keels ride on thy tide—
A thousand keels and more ;
They bear the spoils of every clime
To England's busy shore.

Each gallant vessel's flag is up,
And streaming in the breeze
Alongside of our noble " Jack,"
The pride of all the seas.

A motley throng they are, indeed,
And lade with every store ;
In search of gain they tempt the deep,
And brave the tempest's roar.

Speed onward well, ye noble crafts,
Let Commerce flourish still ;
Her fleets are manned by heroes true,
Though no man's blood they spill.

Go plough the waves, ye gallant barques,
And range the world free ;
Nor rest until your noble keels
Have rippled every sea.

—◇—

Verses

*On receiving from England a Bunch of Violets sent by a young English
Lady, whom I had never seen. (They were Faded on Arrival.)*

HAIL, faded violets, token fair,
From merry England sent,
Where once in bloom and beauty rare
You breathed sweet perfume on the air,
But now, alas ! 'tis spent.

Once pressed by gentle maiden's hand,
    You did her bosom deck ;
Then doubly welcome to this land
To one of Poesy's tuneful band,
    For that sweet maiden's sake.

The maiden young by whom you're sent
    My fancy paints her fair ;
And in her bosom must be pent
Those kindred fires divinely lent—
    Romance and Love, sweet pair.

Such treasured gift from far away
    Might well my bosom fire,
To bid the winds that round me play
To that fair maiden bear away
    The thought her flowers inspire.

But, oh ! the winds so fickle blow—
    Too fickle far for me--
They'd toss my message to and fro ;
So I shall wait, though time is slow,
    Until herself I see.

The Spirit of Freedom.

WHO hears not in the rushing voice
    Of mountain torrents strong,
    The spirit of the land rejoice
    In wild majestic song,
As rushing from the mighty hills
    In foam they seek the sea ;
A rapture wild my bosom fills
    To think I am as free.

Who sees the giant mountains stand
In gloom and grandeur bare,
But sees the spirit of the land
Enthroned in freedom there ?
Like eagle o'er each soaring peak
A sentinel she sails,
Far 'mong the clouds where thunders speak
She rides upon the gales.
She stirs the patriot's heart to feel
Devotion for his land,
And when he meets the foeman's steel
She nerves with power his hand.
She fires the hearts of Bards to sing
In Freedom's glorious strains ;
And stirs the cowering slave to fling
Aside his hated chains,
And rise in might and boldly fight,—
" A Freeman of the Lord,"
Nor cease until he sheath with right
" His own triumphant sword."

The Grandeur of Labour.

YE carping cynics, who despondent rove,
Thro' life in misery, devoid of love,
Thro' earth a wilderness of toil and tears,
Of death and sorrow thro' the fleeting years,
Uplift your heads of woe and view the scene
Of earth resplendent in its robe of green—
A globe of beauty 'neath the azure span ;
Heaven made thee lord of it, O ! God like man.
Then, shame upon the ingrate wretch so base
As whine, in misery, away his days ;
H

Up! earth awaits us and invites our hand
To change the desert to a fruitful land.
Health shines upon the rugged brow of toil,
Strong is the arm that wrestles with the soil;
A noble independence in the bosom glows,
To reap the fields that honest labour sows.
Heaven said, by labour shall thy bread be won,
In sweating brow until thy race is run ;
Such Heaven's law—true blessing in disguise—
As witness rustic health, with beaming eyes.
The hardy, vigour of the peasant's lot
Enshrines in happiness his humble cot ;
No pampered luxury his manhood stains,
Or blights his days with idle folly's pains.
No vices enervate his hardy frame ;
And virtue's precepts from the sire and dame
The children learn in their early days,
And, guileless, follow in their parents' ways.
While blessed freedom over cot and hall
Keeps sacred vigil 'gainst oppression's thrall,
A glorious beacon of divinest light,
Whose beam annihilates dark slavery's night ;
A common freedom is our common dower,
We owe no homage to that despot power
That robs existence of its dearest charm,
And idly eats the fruit of labour's arm.

The Tartan.

COME, Scottish men, an' Scottish maids,
　　Put on your tartan kilts an' plaids,
　An' deck yoursel's wi' braw cockades,
　　An' stand up for the tartan.

Let foreign birkies gape an' stare
At Scotland's sons in garb sae rare,
We still will laugh at them, an' wear
    Our warld-famous Tartan.

It is the garb our fathers wore
Wi' patriot pride in days o' yore,
An' won on many a foreign shore
    Bright honours in the Tartan.

Upon the field o' Waterloo,
When bullets thick as hailstones flew,
Our plaided pipers loudly blew
    To cheer the lads in Tartan.

An' when the Cavalry o' France
In floods o' valour did advance,
In vain their fiery steeds did prance
    Around our squares o' Tartan.

The Scottish lads in close array
Stood man to man upon that day,
And thick as leaves the Frenchmen lay
    Around our squares o' Tartan.

Thrice glorious garb o' Scotland brave,
For ever let the tartan wave;
'Tis Freedom's flag, for ne'er a slave
    E'er wore the bonnie Tartan.

Come rally then frae Tweed to Spey,
Ye Scottish lads an' lasses gay,
An' wi' one voice declare for aye
    To still preserve the Tartan.

Holiday Song.

ADIEU for a time to the roar of the street,
    With its hustle and bustle of hurrying feet,
     Where the chorus of traffic for ever doth ring—
"Gold! gold! I am making from everything."

Adieu to the city, to commerce good-bye,
And ho for the land of the mountains so high!
Already in fancy the heath I can see
In glory that springs by the rush of the Dee.

Already its health-breathing perfume I smell;
O! sweet is its odour, and free is the gale
That's stirring the leaves in the forests of Mar,
And chasing the mists over dark Lochnagar.

Then onward speed quickly, thou monster of steam,
That lights up the darkness with bosom agleam,
And shoots through the night with the speed of the
    gale—
Oh, swift is the rush of the Limited Mail.

Now just as the grey of the morning appears
The City of Granite its turrets uprears,
Asleep by the ocean. O, welcome the sight!
My bosom is thrilled at the view with delight.

For few now the miles to be run e'er I meet
The fond ones awaiting my coming to greet;
And soon will I enter with pleasure the home
Where so happy I lived e'er I learned to roam.

—◇—

Farewell, Old Scotia.

FAREWELL, old Scotia, wild and grand,
    Proud birthplace of my sires;

The leaving of thine honoured strand
  This parting song inspires.

Farewell, each dear, familiar scene,
  That I awhile have known;
Thy memory I shall cherish green
  When far from thee I've gone.

Sweet bonds of love, unite my heart
  To Scotland and my home;
For "Auld Lang Syne" can joys impart
  To Scots, where'er they roam.

The woody glens, and soaring hills,
  And burnies wimpling clear,
The absent Scotchman's bosom fills
  With memories ever dear.

I go not to the golden West,
  The foaming ocean o'er,
Nor do I seek my course to haste
  To Afric's arid shore.

The task's not mine to seek for wealth,
  In distant, sunless caves;
Nor mine the need to hunt for health
  Upon the glittering waves.

A bardic son of commerce I,
  And here amid the strife
Of cities, with their turrets high,
  I note the tide of life.

And on this tide the man must float,
  Who lives amid the throng,
With little time to raise the note
  Of sad or joyous song.

Then, for a time, to thee, farewell,
    Proud birthplace of my sires ;
I mighty London soon shall hail,
    With all its thousand spires.

But, dear old Scotia, wild and grand,
    I hope again to view,
When I shall bid the stranger's land
    A lasting, long adieu.

The Forest Camp.

THROUGH the forest, dark and dreary,
    Wailed the wind with solemn moan,
And the tented sleepers, weary,
    Heard the canvas flap and groan ;
Heard it through their fitful sleeping
    Like the distant thunder's boom,
For their soul's were vigil keeping,
    Conscious of impending doom ;
And the reedy tent pole quivered
    In each fibre, as the gale
Gusty blow on blow delivered
    On its canvas coat of mail.
Eerie shone the embers dying,
    Red and lurid, in the gloom,
And the night birds' dreary crying
    Screeched like ghouls around a tomb.
Weirdly in that midnight lonely,
    Through the pall of blackest night,
Shone those dying embers only
    With a dim and ghostly light ;
And anon with sickly shiver,
    Shooting up, a sudden glare

Lit the gloom with phantom quiver
  Ere expiring in the air,
While, like eyes of demons staring
  From the depths of darkest hell,
Indian eyes in wrath were glaring
  On the sleepers' faces pale.
Grimly as the fiends of fable
  Scowled those eyes with savage glow—
Scowled as Cain had scowled on Abel,
  When he struck the murderer's blow.
O'er each silent sleeper dreaming
  Coldly gleamed a scalping knife;
Down they flashed, and each was streaming
  With the heart's blood of a life.
Then like dusky phantom's gliding,
  Soft the Indians passed in haste,
Through the forest, swiftly striding,
  To their wigwams in the west.
Peaceful sleep those murdered hunters
  By the rushing Delawarr,
Through the summers and the winters,
  In the shady forest far.
By the banks of that broad river,
  In the soil that makes its shore,
Silently they rest for ever,
  And the Indians are no more.

—◇—

Morning Beauties.

WHEN the early tints of morning
    Tinge the skies with roseate hue,
  And the flowers, the earth adorning,
    Smile beneath the crystal dew;

When the little larks are singing
  Merrily high in the blue,
And the woodlands green are ringing
  With the mellow music too—
Then the waking soul of Nature
  Whispers to the heart of man ;
Bids him note her legislature—
  Bids him view her wondrous plan.
Love and peace and beauty mingle
  As they limn the matchless scene,
Weaving flowers adown the dingle—
  Nature's woof of fairest sheen.
Man, the " lord " of the creation,
  Here may feast his noble mind ;
But full joy and consolation
  Here he vainly seeks to find.
In the eyes of winsome maiden,
  Sparkling fair as stars above ;
In her lips, with laughter laden,
  Lie the sources of his love.
There his bliss and solace mingle,
  And from thence his sorrows flow ;
Strange is man, and strange is woman—
  Each to each a joy and woe.

By the Sea.

WHEN I see the ocean breakers
  Beat along the rocky shore,
    I delight to hear the music
  Of their hollow sounding roar;
And to watch the curling waves
  As, with crests of snowy white,
They recede to gather volume,
  And advance again in might.

And away where sky and ocean
  Seem to blend their blue in one
Floats a speck upon the waters
  Which the eye can barely scan.
But as distance fades it rises
  To the view a swelling sail
Of some gallant merchant vessel
  Coming on before the gale.
It rides the heaving waters
  Like a thing of life; in pride
Flinging back the foamy billows
  As they leap upon its side;
And with snowy sails distended,
  Like some seabird, skims along
To the music, 'mong the cordage,
  Of the ocean breezes' song.
Blow, blow, ye ocean breezes, blow,
  And fill the noble sail
Of the barque of golden commerce,
  When 'tis spread to catch the gale
No armed warriors throng its deck,
  Its peaceful flag, unfurled,
Flies stainless, free, on every sea,
  The highway of the world.

The Rain.

HEAR the dashing and the splashing
  Of the dreary winter rain,
    As it lashes, as it splashes,
O'er the dripping window-pane.
Dashing, lashing washing, splashing,
  O'er the dripping window-pane.
Oh! the weary patter, patter,
  Of the dreary winter rain.

In the morning hear it dashing,
  At the noonday hear it still,
As it rushes, as it gushes,
  O'er the flooded window-sill.
Dashing, lashing, washing, splashing,
  O'er the flooded window-sill,
In a never-ceasing current
  That might drive a little mill
With the volume of its torrent
  Pouring like a little rill,
With a weary patter, patter,
  O'er the flooded window-sill.
Morning, evening, night, and noonday,
  All the day, and all the night,
From the dawning to the twilight,
  From the eve till morning light.
Dashing, lashing, washing, splashing,
  From the eve till morning light,
Ever falling, falling, falling
  In its dreary, downward flight;
Dancing, glancing in its falling
  To the left and to the right,
Floating, floating all around us
  In a thousand bubbles bright.
Hear the watery voices calling
  From the river in its might,
Seaward pouring, wildly roaring,
  Like a demon in affright,
Lashed to turbulence and madness,
  In a devastating main,
Rushing o'er the plain and meadow,
  O'er the meadow and the plain.
Oh! the weary patter, patter
  Of the dreary winter rain.

The Lover's Star.

WHEN nature wakes to joyous birth
   And robes the forest trees in green,
      With wealth of blossom decks the earth,
And crowns with springing flow'rs the scene.
'Tis sweet to view the dewy morn,
   When tuneful laverocks pipe their lay
On quivering wing, still upward borne,
   To greet the rosy ope of day.

But sweeter 'tis at evening hour,
   When nature all is hushed in rest,
To woo in some secluded bower
   The bonnie lass that ye lo'e best.
With none to witness but the star
   That twinkles through the twilight grey,
Diffusing from its place afar
   The lover's light at close of day.   ·

Belovéd star, beneath thy beam,
   When love's emotions swell the heart,
Youth knows its first and sweetest dream,
   With all the bliss it can impart.
Then welcome ever, evening star,
   When twilight shadows gather grey,
Diffusing from thy place afar
   The lover's light at close of day.

—◇—

The Dying Day.

THE dying day, the dying day, behold its glorious
   close;
The west reflects in living fire the orange and
   rose,

As slowly down heaven's archéd steep the setting sun
  is rolled,
A flaming sphere of radiant light, a ball of burnished
  gold.
This is the closing of a day that beautiful hath been;
No lowering clouds have crossed the sky or dimmed
  the azure scene;
But like a life of tranquil calm the hours have passed
  away,
Oh, may *our* closing hours be bright as those of
  dying day.
How swiftly have the moments fled since at the rosy
  dawn
The world awoke to life and work—'tis but a little
  span;
And such is life, a fleeting day beneath the arch of
  heaven;
Pray, may we catch and use aright the moments that
  are given.
I've seen the day awake in storm and sink in beauty
  calm;
And winds that at the morning roared ere eve be soft
  as balm;
And days that broke in glory fair have died in storm
  and gloom;
How like, alas! our human birth; alas! how like
  our tomb.
We wake to life in innocence, and shout with childish
  glee
To vent the joy within our hearts while yet they're
  young and free,
Life's darksome clouds are yet afar; its skies are
  azure blue;
Its storms are sleeping in repose, all hid from human
  view;
And while we wander pilgrim-like this troubled
  earthly sphere,

Like to a day of summer hours may life to us appear.
But, be it storm, or sun, or gloom, pray, when we
pass away,
The end may be as beautiful as summer's dying day.

—◇—

Charms of Nature.

THERE'S a charm, my love, in the Springtime,
When the early flowers appear,
When the groves are filled with music
And the skies grow blue and clear.
When the skies grow blue and clear, my love,
And the groves with music ring,
But the light of thine eyes, my darling,
To me is eternal Spring.

There's a charm, my love, in the Summer,
With its richer, brighter glow,
When the winds are soft and balmy
And the waters murmur low ;
When the waters murmur low, my love,
And the winds blow soft and free,
But thy voice and thy smile, my darling,
Have a sweeter charm for me.

There's a charm, my love, in the Autumn,
When the forest leaves grow brown,
When the fields are stripped of harvest,
And the Summer birds are flown ;
When the Summer birds are flown, my love,
And the harvest fields are bare,
But thy fairy form, my darling,
A changeless charm doth wear.

There's a charm, my love, in the winter
When the snowflakes whirl around,

And diamonds of frost in thousands
Are gemming the crispy ground ;
Are gemming the crispy ground, my love,
And glistening everywhere,
But Nature's charms, my darling,
With thine can never compare.

A Northern Sunset.

MARK the golden glow of sunset
    Shoot the western hills along,
        Kindling o'er their crest a radiance
        Worthy of Promethian song.
Glorious gleam those fiery lances,
    And the clouds, with crimson dress't,
Hang like banners of an army
    Marching to the flaming West.
Under them the azure ocean
    Rolls as he has ever done ;
Waiting with a restless bosom
    To embrace the sinking sun.

Spring.

THE snows are all vanished, the biting frost's
        banished—
    Forget now the winter so drear.
All Nature rejoices ; come mingle your voices
    To welcome the Queen of the year.

Now flow'rets are springing, and birds gaily singing
    'Mid groves that are all budding green ;
For Spring light and airy is here like a fairy,
    Adorning with beauty the scene.

Now sweethearts are walking, and hopefully talking
  Of things in the future to be.
In the spring-time of life happy visions are rife
  As daisies that spangle the lea.

The Spring brings us gladness and banishes sadness,
  As snows 'fore its breath disappear ;
For the cuckoo's first call is a signal to all
  That the blooms of the summer are near.

The Summer is coming, with honey bees humming
  Their song to the nectarous flower ;
And amorous cooing of cushats a-wooing
  Soft floating from forest and bower.

Sweet Summer all mellow and Autumn's deep yellow,
  They all have their pleasures I ween,
And the " beautiful snow " in its season I lo'e,
  But Spring with its blossoms is Queen.

—◇—

Spring Song.

RETURNING spring by bank and brae
    Is weaving flowery garlands gay,
    And tinting green each budding spray.
    O vernal spring ! O beauty !

Sweet in the early morning clear
The jovial ploughman's song to hear,
As o'er the fields his harrows steer
    With merry clatter clanking.

He sees on yonder winding stream
The rays of morning sunlight gleam
As shadow glimmer in a dream.
    O vernal spring ! O beauty !

How fair to see the yellow grain
Fall in the ground like golden rain !
And spring to life and light again
    With promise of full harvest.

And fair and fresh is earth to see
When Nature's subtle witchery
Hath touched thy cords of melody,
    O vernal spring ! O beauty !

Leave now the city's sombre gloom,
Leave now the workshop and the loom,
And woo to hollow cheeks the bloom
    That spring is freely showering.

Drink deep delight when she is here,
Breathe health beneath her skies so clear,
Fair herald of the leafy year,
    O vernal spring ! O beauty

—◇—

Spring.

AS forth I wander, round my feet
    The early flowers are springing sweet ;
    And wild birds sing on every spray
Their love in gushing, warbled lay.

The breath of spring is in the air,
Its mystic spell is everywhere ;
The hawthorn blossoms, milky white,
Are bursting to the sunny light.

The corn is springing from the clod ;
The lowly gowan adorns the sod,
Wet with the pearly dew so clear,
That sparkle like sweet maiden's tear.

In silvery cascades from the hills,
With song pour down the limpid rills,
To swell the river's opaque tides,
As, seaward, stately on it glides.

'Tween banks adorned with greening woods
That wave above the darkling floods,
And stoop to kiss the passing wave
Ere yet 'tis lost in ocean grave.

The bees buzz by in greedy haste
The sweets of clover'd leas to taste,
To sip the nectar from the flowers—
Improving still the sunny hours.

Sweet spring! thou cheer'st the hearts of men,
And brings them joys of youth again,
With memories sweet of bygone years,
Which lapse of time but more endears.

—◇—

A Springtime Song.

SWEET it is to muse and listen
    In the Springtime of the year,
  When the early blossoms glisten,
    And the song of birds we hear;
But far sweeter than the blossoms
    Or the birdies as they sing
Are the thoughts that rise within us
    At the dawning of the Spring.

For the summer-day is coming
    We have waited for so long,
With its flowers of fuller blossom
    And its birds of sweeter song.

I

Oh ! our winter night of sadness
    Is now passing fast away,
And the dawning of our gladness
    Cometh with our summer day.

Courage then ye hearts though weary,
    For the brighter days in store
Soon shall chase away the dreary
    From your lives for ever more.
For a fairer morn is glowing
    Close behind the shadows grey,
And the souls in grief now bowing
    Shall be glad and rest for aye.

April.

NOO April has come wi' its sunshine an' showers—
    Its wealth o' spring blossoms adornin' the
        bowers,
An' sweetly the birdies sing through the bright
    hours
    To welcome it blithely again.

An' Nature arrayed in its mantle o' green,
Bespangled wi' flow'rets sae bonnie, I ween,
Smiles sweetly, an' calls us to view the glad scene,
    An' welcome sweet April again.

When ilk blade in the gloamin' is wet wi' the dew,
To see the young couples sae dearly I lo'e,
As they tell the auld story that ever is new
    O' their love in sweet April again.

The dove in the forest is croonin' o' love,
An' the birds swell the chorus in ilka green grove,

An' surely our young hearts a-wooin' should rove,
For this is sweet April again.

E'en old hearts are glad as they think o' the day
When in spring time o' life they hae wander'd sae
    gay,
An' still as they think o' that time far away
They welcome sweet April again.

You're welcome, sweet April, wi' sunshine an' showers,
An' wealth o' spring blossoms adornin' the bowers,
An' birds singin' blithely through a' the bright hours—
You're welcome, thrice welcome again.

—◇—

Flowery May.

WELCOME, sweet and flowery May,
    With thy sunshine and thy showers,
Singing birds on every spray,
    Floral wreaths and vernal bowers.
Summer zephyrs soft and light
    Stir the clovers on the lea,
Nodding plumes of red and white
    Bearing each a honey bee.
Laverocks soar on dewy wing
    To greet with song the rosy morn ;
Sweetest month of all the ring—
    Firstling child of summer born,
'Neath thy footsteps daisies spring,
    Bank and brae are clad with flowers,
And with song the forests ring
    Through the bright and sunny hours.
Welcome, sweet and flowery May,
    With thy sunshine and thy showers,
Singing birds on every spray,
    Floral wreaths and vernal bowers.

Leafy June.

'TIS June, and all the bursting buds
    Have flung their life in leaves around,
And earth all green in flowery sheen
    Is vocal with the murmurous sound

Of waters soft and pipes of birds
    That gushing trill from earliest morn
From out the groves of living green,
    And from the milky blossomed thorn.

The first sweet breath of kindly air
    That bade the birds begin to sing
Like magic floated o'er the land,
    And work the pulses of the spring.

Sweet April nurtured with her showers
    The wealth of bloom that decked the May,
Whose fragrance woo'd with subtle power
    The lingering swallows far away.

And brought them borne on lightning wings,
    From where the summers linger aye,
To flit among our northern scenes
    Like spirits of a transient day.

So doth the June-time of our lives
    Burst forth in sunshine and in leaves,
But may our autumn's cooler hours
    Show wealth of fruit and golden sheaves

In goodly store, to cheer our hearts
    When life's December winds shall moan,
The labourer shall have his hire,
    The fruitless nought to rest upon.

Autumn.

NOW Autumn's mellow hues are seen
　By forests fields and glades,
　　Commingling with the summer's green
　　Their russet tinted shades.
The hills and moors with heather bloom
　Are purple far and wide,
And yellow are the braes with broom
　In all its golden pride.
O'erhead the soft and azure sky
　Looks on earth's fields below,
Where ripened barley, oats, and rye
　Wave rustling to and fro.
And soon the sons of rustic toil,
　With sinewy arms strong,
Will gladly on the laden soil
　To harvest labour throng.
For smiling plenty 'mong the grain,
　As bounty's queen arrayed,
Invites the mowers forth again
　To reap her stores of bread.
For He the harvest Lord on high
　Hath blessed the corn and wheat,
That beasts of earth and birds that fly
　And men may live and eat.

—◇—

My Sailor Boy.

OH! where is my sailor boy, Oh! where?
　The night is wild and the murky clouds
　　Drive darkly and drear athwart the air
　Like banners of death or inky shrouds.
Is he far, where bounding billows roar
　And toss their spray on the darksome night,

Hissing in wrath like a hell so hoar,
   Or smiting the ship with demon might?

I see the lightning with blinding glare,
   Like tongues of fire flash over the sea,
Rending the pall of the midnight air
   And coiling in flaming serpentry.
Oh! God of the tempest keep my boy
   Wherever to-night his course may be,
And bring him again, my life and joy,
   My truant wanderer back to me.

How many mothers on bended knee
   Look out to-night o'er the waters wild,
Praying the Stiller of Galilee
   To keep some truant and wandering child.
How many sorrowing hearts of love
   Look out o'er the world's ocean drear,
And pray to the kindly Watch above
   To keep some wandering loved one dear,

Wherever those wandering loved ones go
   Bring them again to the path aright
That leads to home from sorrow and woe,
   And still the cry of those hearts to-night—
Where is my child the loved and lost,
   Where is my child, Oh! where?

———◇———

Love's Eden.

BY yon wide and winding river,
   Where the wild birds warble ever,
   Sweetest songs that swell and quiver
     Fraught with melodie,
There are bowers for ever green,
Fairest flowers of brightest sheen,

Where I wander with my queen
  Fondly, joyfullie.

Blue and clear the skies above
Bending o'er the scene of love,
And the cooing of the dove
  Blends harmoniouslie
With the murmuring river grand
As its waters lave the strand,
While together mute we stand
  List'ning rapturouslie.

At the close of summer's day
While the red sun far away,
Wrapt in clouds of gold and grey,
  Sinking peacefulie,
Sheds his lingering rosy beams
O'er this Eden of our dreams,
Flushing all with ruddy gleams;
  Love's soft witcherie

Weaves its glamour evermore,
Till this flower-bespangled shore
'Neath the notes the warblers pour
  Forth unceasinglie,
Seems the sweet enchanted strand
Of some fairy haunted land
Opening to love's magic wand
  Unresistinglie.

Paradise from mortals shriven,
Back to men is freely given,
Love, the sweetest rose of heaven,
  Earth's felicitie.
In each bosom let it bloom,
Flower of light dispelling gloom,
Every heart hath vacant room
  For this rosarie.

I shall aye by yonder river,
Where the wild birds warble ever,
Sweetest songs that swell and quiver
    Fraught with melodie,
Wander ever with my queen
'Mong the bowers for ever green,
'Mong the flowers of fairest sheen,
    Foudly, joyfullie.

—◆—

Nonsense.

IF you have seen the golden glory
    Of a sunset in the west,
  Or the sparkle of a brooklet
  Running in its childish haste;
Or the ship in storm careering
    Through the ocean's wild abyss,
Or a beauteous maiden sleeping,
    Tempting theft of secret kiss;
Or the summer roses wither
    'Fore the breath of autumn's blast,
Swaying in their dying beauty,
    Perfume shed, and glory past.
If you have seen all these, good reader,
    Gazed on them with optic keen,
As an eagle from his eyry,
    Bless me! what a deal you've seen.

—◆—

Boldie.

(A Canine Friend.)

MY Boldie dog, I like you weel;
    Mair sense you hae than mony a chiel,

An' weel I ken your love is real,
    For you've nae guile,
Nae frien' wi' heart mair warm an leal
    I've seen this while.

Unlike the frien's o' human race,
Nae smile can light your honest face;
But, lad, I like you nane the less,
    For weel I ken
A smile aft hides a heart that's base
    'Mang fellowmen.

Your glossy coat o' black an' white
Is aye to me a welcome sight;
It fits you like a glove sae tight
    Frae nose to tail;
An' keeps you warm by day an' night
    Frae weather snell.

An', Boldie lad, you're aye the same;
The fashion's play wi' you nae game;
While folks may hap baith back and wame
    In garments new
O' mony a rare an' foreign name,
    An' rarer hue,

You jog alang frae year to year,
Your glossy coat nae waur o' wear;
To frien's an' strangers you appear
    Just what you are—
An honest dog that kens nae fear
    'Neath sun or star.

A faithfu' loon my Boldie dog,
Swift can you run by brae or bog
To turn a rangin' coo or hog
    When they wad stray,

An' hale an' hardy may you jog
    For mony a day.

An' when you dee, my honest frien',
I'll lay you 'neath the sward sae green,
An' ower your head I'll raise a stane
    To mark the grave
O' ane that has mair usefu' been,
    Mair true an' brave,

Than mony a man wha boasts a soul,
Yet wanders to his earthly goal
Wi' heart as black an' hard's a coal
    That winna burn,
Less honoured than the very mole
    That haunts his urn.

—◇—

The Jolly Tailor.

(With the author's respects to Tammas Bodkin.)

I AM a jolly tailor, O!
    Belongin' to the Border,
'Mong high an' low, where'er I go
    My needle's aye in order.
Some people ca' me "whip-the-cat"
    Because I hae nae station,
But fient a thread care I for that—
    I like my occupation.

My father was a decent man,
    A farmer an' a beadle,
But I preferred to diggin' lan'
    The diggin' wi' my needle.
An' though at times I maun confess
    My livin' is but chancy,

I win my way in ilka place
  By needle necromancy.

Wi' wife an' maid, where'er I ca',
  There's aye some thing needs stitchin',
Sae frae its case I quickly draw
  My needle sae bewitchin',
An' divin' it into the clout,
  Right up an' down I send it,
An' never stop to look about
  Until the job is endit.

O, weel I like to see a hole—
  A hole that's needin' stitchin'—
To let me at it, by my soul,
  I'm often fairly itchin'.
I winna sew at orra claith—
  Sic stuff, I'd rather want it—
For ance or twice, upon my aith,
  My needle has been blunted.

The thread's sae strong I keep on han'
  'Twad moor a fleet o' whalers,
Or in a storm pull to lan'
  A score o' drownin' sailors.
The first o' it, sae stout an' lang
  (This is nae Eastern fable),
Was used the scaffoldin' to hang
  About the "Tower o' Babel."

I also am a doctor quack,
  An' cleverly can tell you
The sort o' medicine to tak'
  If anything should ail you.
In head or wame if you hae pain
  Just drink a merry jorum,
An' dance for several oors on en'
  The Reel o' Tullochgorum.

Although I'm but a "whip the cat"
  You may believe my story,
I give it free, it's cheap at that,
  I only get the glory.
An' by my "goose" that's in the fire,
  It's fushionless to feed on,
A feckless diet to retire
  To bed an' chaw your queed on.

Amid the war o' human life
  I keep my needle prickin';
There's blunter weapons i' the strife—
  I've little fear o' stickin'.
Should e'er my needle an' my thread
  Bring Fortune, I will hail her;
But still content wi' daily bread,
  I'll range a jolly tailor.

—◇—

The Traveller.

AWAY where the pine tree cleaves the sky
  On the soaring Alpine summits high,
  Where the daring eagle has his home,
And the mountain flocks fleet-footed roam,
A traveller lone from his path did stray,
For the mist hung heavy o'er his way,
And no friendly beam its radiance gave
To light the path of the wanderer brave,—
For a wanderer brave, indeed, was he
Who had ranged the world, land and sea,
From the foamy ocean's liquid deeps,
To the mountain glacier's shining steeps.
He had seen the snows that gird the Pole
Where the hungry bear did fiercely growl,
And the Northern lights did brightly stream
Fantastic in their varying gleam.

He had heard the jungle's voices rise
In a chorus wild 'neath Afric's skies,
When the beasts of prey their victims rent
In the darksome hour that midnight lent.
He had been where tropic warblers sing,
And the shelt'ring palms their shadows fling.
When the noonday sun doth fiercely glare,
And the flowers with perfume fill the air.
He had looked on skies of azure blue,
And had slept beneath the deadly dew,
And beheld the sultry lightnings flash
Where Orient thunders roll and crash.
And now, astray on this Alpine height,
'Mid mist and gathering shades of night,
He wildly gropes; but he gropes in vain,
For he'll ne'er see morning light again.
A slip, a fall, and the wanderer brave
In his swift descent no hand can save;
'Mong the rocks his mangled body lay
For the royal eagle's feast next day ;
And his whitened bones a peasant found,
And o'er them he reared a rocky mound
To mark the sight of the nameless tomb
'Mid those silent Alpine crags of gloom.

---♦---

The Irish Exile.

AN exile of Erin, with heart sad and heavy,
    Sat lone by the sea where the wild breakers
        foam;
Bedimmed with emotion, his eye swept the ocean
To Ireland, the land of his nation and home.
"Oh ! Erin," he cried, as the fast rolling tear fell,
"Erin, my native, bright isle of the sea,

May Heaven protect thee, and shield thy green
　　bosom—
Green as thy memory for ever shall be.
The fame of thy heroes shall flourish undying ;
Remember, them, Eriu, remember thy brave
Who lived and who died for thy cause and thy freedom,
Defying oppression to make thee a slave.
I'm longing to see thy green hills and thy valleys .
By clear running Shannon, where childhood I spent ;
How oft by its banks with my darling I've wandered,
When love to my bosom sweet ardour hath lent.
Now, far from the land of my childhood, I wander
An exile from Eriu, my pride and my home ;
No more but in fancy can I cross the ocean
To wander the green banks of Shannon upon."
The prayer of the exile for thee nightly rises,
As, lone by the sea where the wild breakers foam,
He looks with emotion to thee o'er the ocean,
Bright Erin, the land of his nation and home.

Caledonia.

O! CALEDONIA dear to me,
　　Thy mist encircled mountains free,
　Thy rushing rivers and thy rills
That winding glance among thy hills,
They all are dear, thrice dear to me—
Famed haunts of love and liberty.
Land of the valorous and brave,
Whose bosom never nursed a slave ;
Land of the tartan far renowned,
With hoary honours girt and crowned,
Thy wandering sons fond turn to thee—
Famed land of love and liberty.

Proud Rome of yore with mailèd hand
Vain strove old Caledonia grand
To fetter in that firm embrace
Whose martial grip bound every race,
But foiled and beaten turned from thee—
Famed land of love and liberty.
In every glen and mountain pass,
On moorland and in wild morass,
The whitened bones of warriors brave
That found a rude untimely grave,
All tell of struggles stern by thee—
Famed land of love and liberty.
May thy wild mountain eagles soar
High o'er the crags still as of yore,
And thy old ruddy lion bold
Glow proudly on his field of gold,
And honest worth aye "bear the gree"
Among thy men and maidens free—
Famed land of love and liberty.

—◆—

Lines on Inkermann.

THE morning dawn had not yet broke,
  And misty vapours clad the hill;
The sleeping camp had not awoke,
  But dreamed of home in silence still.
Dream on, ye sleepers, while you may,
  Your life and dreams will soon be o'er;
For many, ere the close of day,
  Will sleep, alas! to wake no more.
Death's hurricane is brooding nigh,
  Though stilled as yet the cannon's roar;
And those green slopes on which you lie
  Will soon be crimsoned with your gore.

Ah! rude awakening, hark the drums
 That loudly call the foe is near;
The whizzing shot proclaims he comes
 To meet those hearts that know no fear.
The pickets backward slowly go,
 Contesting inch by inch the way;
While regiments press to meet the foe,
 And mingle in the bloody fray.
The gleaming steel is red with blood,
 While flies around the death-winged lead;
And friend and foe writhe in that flood
 Of crimson, on one awful bed;
Till vanquished Russia fled these slopes,
 Piled with the ghastly heaps of slain,
Stretched stark with all their perished hopes
 To wait the last grand Bugle's strain.

—◇—

The River of Death.

DEATH as a ghastly boatman rows,
 And this darksome river ever flows,
 And a chilly wind forever blows
  Where he steers his laden barque.
The river's brink is bleak and bare,
And a motley crowd are waiting there,
In holy calm or wild despair,
  For the pilot pale and grim
Silently dips the muffled oar
Bearing them to the unseen shore,
And the boatman deeply chants "no more
  Do you e'er return again."
And the hand of Time is mowing,
And the barque is ever rowing
On this tide forever flowing
  In a current cold and dark.

Maggie Bella.

MANY are the pretty babies
        Of both sexes I have seen,
    But of all the many babies
Maggie Bella is the queen.
May she grow in grace and beauty
With the round of fleeting years,
And perform true woman's duty
In this vale of sin and tears.
Like her charming graceful mother,
With her bright and fairy eyes,
She will cause some lad to smother
In his bosom love-sick sighs.
May the sun shine bright above her,
Making life eternal spring,
Guardian spirits round her hover,
And all virtues to her cling.
Darling girl, may health still deck her
With its bright and rosy glow,
Nor the tide of bliss forsake her,
But in growing volume flow.
Maggie Bella, rosebud tender,
Yet to grace some nuptial bower,
May all joys in life attend her
And sweet peace her closing hour.

Sons of Britain.

SONS of Britain, gather, gather,
        Round the standard of the brave,
    That a thousand years has floated
Victor over land and wave.
By the mighty deeds of valour

J

That of old our fathers wrought
On a thousand fields of battle
Where in Freedom's cause they fought.
Should a foreign foeman venture
E'er to land on Britain's shore,
Hearts of oak he'll find undaunted
To oppose him as of yore.
Still our gallant fleet is floating,
Thunder clad on every sea,
Still our gallant flag is flying
Emblem of the brave and free.
The flag that o'er Trafalgar floated
When the Frenchman was laid low,
While a Britain lives to guard it
Ne'er shall strike to foreign foe.
And while Caledonia's pibroch
Pours its war note on the blast
Highland lads from glen and mountain
As of yore shall gather fast.
Who can stand before the on-rush
Of the dreaded British steel?
Swept before our ranks of valour
Foes of Britain backward reel.
Or in squares all bayonet crested
Vain is fiery horseman's shock,
Back they roll like waves of ocean,
Broken on the mighty rock.
Land of freemen, land of heroes,
Girt about with ocean wave,
Flourish ever, fade thee never,
Home of beauty and the brave.

—◇—

More Coals.
(A LODGER'S REVERIE).

WHEN we sit and deeply ponder
In the twilight all alone,

And in fancy backward wander
Through the happy years long gone ;
When in long array before us
Faded memories dimly glow,
Like the shadows flitting near us
In the corner to and fro ;
When perchance some face is smiling
Through the mists of many a year,
With a look that's quite beguiling—
Yes, a look remembered dear ;
And our bosom like the ocean
Swells in ecstacy of bliss,
As we think with sweet emotion
On that last angelic kiss ;
When thus lost in contemplation
'Tis so bitter to our souls,
When some one with animation
Shouts, sir do you need more coals.

—◇—

Britain's Seamen.

YE seamen of Old Britain bold,
    Whose home is on the deep,
Who ride upon the stormy wave
And through the tempests sweep ;
Who throng your decks in danger's hour
At duty's noble call,
With cheers ye welcome victory
Or deathless glory's pall.
Ye daring spirits of the deep,
Inheritors of fame,
Transmitted from your fathers,
Ye still uphold their name ;
And twined among their laurels

Your honours brightly shine,
Increasing more the lustre
Of their heroic line.
Ye wear them all unsullied,
Ye Ocean warrior's bold,
And show the world that Britain
Is Britain still of old.
And while on high your battle flag .
Streams proudly in the breeze,
Britannia ever shall be called
The Monarch of the seas.
And while the years in cycles run,
Your deeds ye ocean braves
Shall still maintain a Briton's boast,
" Britannia rules the waves."

— —

After a Jealous Moment.

LOVE, 'tis over now, excuse me,
   Pardon sure you'll ne'er refuse me,
   Cause of all this sad commotion
Was of course my deep devotion.
Jealousy doth walk the ramparts,
Sentinel o'er youthful sweethearts,
Breathing tales he should not mention,
Keeping love still at high tension.
Miser feels not more of pleasure
'Mid his store of golden treasure
Than this rascal feels to tease us
With his sting whene'er he pleases.
Once for all I mean to bind him,
And if I again should find him
Telling tales to spoil my wooing,
As the knave's been lately doing,
I shall give him transportation

To some distant foreign station,—
Say that blissful Isle of Tories,
Cyprus—where he'll no more bore us.
There he'll find some " eastern question "
To improve his bad digestion,
Making Greek and Turkish quarrels,
Sighting fleets and rifle barrels.
There no lovers he torment will,
Or their petty fears foment still
With the ever ready speeches
He in mischief gratis teaches.
Let him mind his " p's and q's,"
Now we know his little ruse,
For, my love, I swear by Venus
He shall come no more between us.

—◇—

Slander.

CHIEF of the bitter ills of life
    That human hearts have wrung
   And widest scattered seeds of strife
   Is Slander's venomed tongue.

Disease and death their victims steal
   When hope and bliss are high,
And fleeting time the wound may heal,
   But Slander cannot die.

The poisoned tale for ever flows
   In stream of darkest stain,
And still recited blacker grows
   As tides by winter's rain.

Oh! wise is he that's slow to speak,
   And speaks but when he's sure,

Unlike to those for mud that seek
   To soil the name that's pure.

If blame there be, then let it rest,
   Nor throw the foremost stone,
The secret griefs the guilty taste,
   For hapless slips atone.

Let golden charity preside
   In heart of man to man—
A light divine to heavenward guide
   Our steps through life's brief span.

Remember Him, who here below
   In meek and lowly guise,
That stooped to stay the tide of woe
   And wipe poor sorrow's eyes.

Did He, the only 'mid the throng
   Who justly could condemn,
Lift up his voice to censure wrong
   And add reproach to shame?

No. Go, He said, and let each deed
   Be better from this hour,
And thus it was the stainéd weed
   He purged to sweetest flower.

The china fine may mock the urn,
   Yet both are simple clay,
Then spiteful venomed babblers spurn
   As reptiles from thy way.

—◇—

Hope.

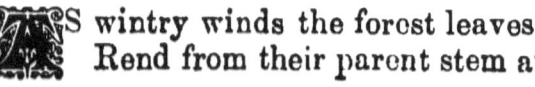

AS wintry winds the forest leaves
   Rend from their parent stem away,

So anguish round the heart still weaves
Despair, when cherished hopes decay.
O, cherished Hope, expectant bliss,
That sweetens all our life below,
All trouble's nought when 'fore our face
We see the still alluring glow.
Friends may prove false, and dark the gloom
Of care and sorrow gather round,
Death bear our treasures to the tomb
And rend the ties that Love had bound;
But still to thee, O! Hope we cling,
Thy cheering whisper bids us know
That Time, with healing in his wing,
Will chase away our night of woe.
Ah! sad indeed the sinking soul
That's shrouded in Despair's dark night,
A chartless bark, without a goal,
Adrift without thy guiding light.
Hope—heavenly pilot on Life's sea
Still steer us with thy angel hand,
Until those golden shores we see
That mark thy bright and native land.

Time.

WHEN o'er this world the sun at first did rise
  And shed his glory from the new made skies,
  He saw creation in its infant form
From centre stretching to the poles of storm.

While heaving seas broke foaming on their strands
Awaking echoes by the silent lands,
Thick-clad with forests in their primal bloom,
Their depths untrodden, unexplored their gloom.

The rivers rising from the hills did sweep
In swelling volume to the mighty deep,
O'er rocks, thro' forests, and thro' vales they rolled
And virgin channels, all unshaped, did mould.

Time then was young,* his eye undimmed by age
Beheld earth's life-scroll an unwritten page;
His sand-glass brimming in his hand held he
To measure cycles of the great To-Be.

Decay and change were written in his gaze,
And dark death followed in his silent pace
To seal his edicts, and to stay the span
Of transitory life to fleeting man.

He saw men grow and spread the world o'er,
And people continents from shore to shore,
Combating Nature with a subtle skill
That bent her powers unto their mighty will.

The savage, groping in the ages dark,
Put forth to ocean in his fragile barque,
And steered for lands, no compass but his mind
To point the shores that Destiny said find.

Still on and upward through the changing years,
Man moving onward his great acmé nears;
His former tools, as toys, are cast aside,
And space is cancelled by his giant stride.

The throbbing engine with its mighty hum
Is but the seedling of a power to come,
While lightning-tongued electric threads extend,
And speak their message to the world's end.

And thus still onward time and change have gone,
And touched with magic every clime and zone,

---

* Time was always; but the reader will understand the simile of Time's
youth as applied to the creation.

O'er seas once ruffled but by wind or tide
Now myriad keels of commerce hourly glide.

'Mid forest wilds now sounds the woodman's stroke
Where nought save Nature ever echo woke,
Those sounds bespeak the forward march of man,
The bugle calls that herald Progress van.

Let Empires rise or wane to their decay,
They're fleeting phantoms of a fleeting day,
Time pregnant with the future sweeps the stage
For coming peoples and a coming age.

The Spectre Boat.

ON yon lake 'mong the hills, when the shades of
night
Have darkened its silvery tide,
A vision is seen in a ghastly light,
Along its lone bosom to glide.
'Tis a boat afloat, and its blood red sail,
Though the winds be hushed and still,
Seems flapped about in some phantom gale,
As it coasts the sable hill.
At the prow there stands a young maiden fair,
With a wild majestic mein,
And her raven hair streams free in air,
And her eye is as eagle's keen.
And her face, as seen in that ghastly light,
Is a face as of the grave,
As the bark glides on in the gloom of night,
O'er the dark and silent wave.
But when morning dawns, and the sunlight bright
Breaks over the waters fair,
They dance and glance in the golden light,
And no spectre boat is there.

Labour's Song.

'TIS not to princes nor to kings
    I owe my royal birth,
  These are but puny gilded things,
I'm monarch of the earth.
O ! strong and sturdy is my arm—
  No limit to its power !
The life that glows within me warm
  Is health and heaven's dower.
I hold no gay and gilded court
  To pamper dissipation,
Nor spend the golden hours in sport
  And idle recreation.
My subjects are yon motley throng,
  With labour's flag unfurled,
Behold them sinewy, brown, and strong,
  The workers of the world.
I till the fruitful spreading fields,
  Reclaim the wastes forlorn,
And garner up when nature yields
  Her stores of wine and corn.
I shape the ship and smooth her deck,
  I guide her o'er the wave,
The first and last in life I make—
  The cradle and the grave.
All things I rule on sea and land,
  Earth's cities are my own,
I fashion with my patent hand
  The scaffold and the throne.
Deep in the drear and sunless mines,
  Where precious stores are resting,
I labour in those dark confines
  Rich spoil from nature wresting.
I stem the seas and bridge the floods
  Of rivers wildly pouring,
And ply my axe 'mid savage woods,

Where angry beasts are roaring.
I urge the engine in its flight
Till earth beneath it trembles,
And light with mystic fire* the night
Till it the day resembles.
With sleeves uprolled I stir the fires,
The world's forges heating—
With sturdy arm, that never tires,
The glowing iron beating,
And though I have no regal train
To win me approbation,
I'm potent king of honest men,
And monarch of creation.

—◇—

The Badge of Blue.

HO ! my lads, come join the legion of the steady
    hearts and true,
Who have bade adieu to Bacchus and put on
the badge of blue.

Fathers, mothers, sisters, brothers, by those precious
souls of thine,
Linger, linger ye no longer o'er the red and rosy wine.

Flee, O flee, that draught of madness—dash the
Devil's dram away;
For the adder soon will sting you, tho' it seems to
sleep to-day.

Sons of time, there is no resting 'twixt the cradle and
the grave ;
Ever, ever onward hasting, wave of life succeeding
wave.

* The Electric Light.

Ere your days are in the shadow, while your lives are
in the flower,
Stretch a hand to help your fellows—"Unity is
strength" and power. .

Let the Poets of the world lend their music's sweetest
notes,
Strong to charm away the serpent coiling round our
brothers' throats.

Shame, alas! on noble manhood lingering 'mong the
drunken crew;
Let his spirit burst its shackles, let him be a hero
true.

Let him boast a noble victory in the purest glory
shrined,
Greater than the great Napoleon is the man that
conquers mind.

His the greatest, grandest Empire, with a brighter
flag unfurled
Than the reddest flag of conquest that has floated
o'er the world.

Who has seen the gin-fiend leering, who has felt his
fetid breath,
But has felt with secret fearing that his fatal hug is
death.

Wrestle with the demon, brothers, wrestle onward
and be brave,
Crush him in his mail and harness deep in dark
oblivion's grave.

Chase him from the cot and palace, and from every
social hearth,

Till the pæan-note of triumph rise from the enfranchised earth.

Ever in the van of progress, Scotia, kingdom of the free,
Point the world's sons and daughters to the path of liberty.

Be thou first to sound the bugle, hardy Scotland meet the foe,
Drive him from thy straths and valleys, and thy hills of virgin snow.

Rally, rally, round our banner, all the good and all the true,
Till from pole to pole the world shall have donned the badge of blue.

—◆—

Youth.

REMEMBERED joys of faded years—
    Years all too quickly that did roll—
Your blissful memory ever cheers
    And lights the labour-weighted soul.

We backward look to that dear time
    When leaves of life were fresh and green;
Youth made the earth a sunny clime
    That had for us no winter keen.

Sweet days of youth, O! season gay—
    Alas! that e'er you should depart—
Thy scenes like swallows round me play,
    And make a summer in my heart.

Where have they gone, the merry hearts
  That shared with us our early joys ?
Now scattered far, they ply the *arts*
  Of peace or war that each employs.

Where are the bright-eyed maidens young,
  The nymphs of youth's enchanting scenes ?
Around them love her charms hath flung,
  And now they reign as household queens.

But backward still to that dear time
  When leaves of life were fresh and green,
They gaze as to a golden clime
  That had for them no winter keen.

Sweet days of youth, O ! season gay,
  'Mid scenes of war or peaceful arts,
Thy joys, like swallows, round us play,
  And make a summer in our hearts.

Memories.

THE skies are bright and blue at noonday,
  And at night the fire-flies glow,
I can see them brightly sparkle
  From my little bungalow,
And amid the bowers of orange
  Sings the bul-bul sweet and clear,
Bringing scenes to my remembrance
  Of that land for ever dear,
Where the mavis and the lintie
  Sweetly lilt their tuneful lays
'Mong the yellow whins and heather
  Far on Scotland's bonnie braes.
Where in childhood I did wander,
  And in manhood I did rove,

Where within my breast was kindled
  First the ardent flame of love.
Now before me they are passing,
  Yes! before me I can see
Youth's companions, now grey-headed ;
  Gladly would they welcome me.
Years of absence make the picture
  To my fancy brightly glow,
As the night reveals the fire-flies
  Sparkling near my bungalow.

—◇—

The Cuckoo.

TO-DAY I heard the cuckoo's note ·
    O'er the greening meadows float
    Waking memories with its strain
Of the vernal Spring again.

When in by-gone happy days,
Romping 'mong the woody braes,
We culled the blushing early flowers
Springing sweet in leafy bowers.

Herald of the balmy Spring
Though no warbled song you sing,
Yet there's music in thy lay
Simple bird of plumage grey.

Spring attends where'er you call,
But when leaves of summer fall
Then to other climes you wing,
There to speak again of Spring.

But where earth is green and fair,
Cuckoo, thou art only there
Waking memories with thy strain
Of the balmy Spring again.

The Soldier's Grave.

WHERE the pines wave dark, and the wood flowers
 spring
 Far away in that southern land,
Round the grave of a soldier the wild roses cling—
 The chief of a warrior band.
A cross rudely cut on the rock by his head
 Marks the spot where his ashes repose,
And long grasses wave o'er his low, narrow bed
 When softly the summer wind blows.
And oft when the sun, sinking red in the west,
 Shed his beam on the soldier's grave,
I have pulled, as I passed by the place of his rest,
 A flower from the bed of the brave.
And though now I am far from that flower-clad grave,
 Yet I often in memory stray
To the rude cut cross by the tomb of the brave,
 In that southern land far away.

The English Maiden's Welcome.

YOU'RE welcome, thrice welcome, sweet rose of
 the south,
 To the land of the heather and broom,
Where cloud-kissing mountains o'ershadow the
 vales
 With their glory, their grandeur, and gloom.

The thistle waves proudly its soft downy plume,
 And the blue-bell adorns the bowers,
And the breezes of Scotland are bracing and free,
 Though they breathe not of southern flowers.

Then welcome, fair daughter of England, we say,
 Fond hearts are awaiting for thee,

To cherish and love you, and make you a home
  In the land of the brave and the free.

Our men are still valiant as heroes of old
  In the conquest of hearts as of land ;
In the glance of their eye fond love you'll descry
  That the heart of no maid can withstand.

But the might of the sword can never compare
  With the arrow of Cupid, I trow ;
For the rose and the thistle now lovingly twine,
  And in beauty together do grow.

A shield and support to each other they prove
  When the tempests around them do rave ;
Then welcome, thrice welcome, sweet rose of the south,
  To the land of the free and the brave.

The Hermit.

IN his hut by the green wood so lonely and wild,
  On a pallet of heath, lay the hermit so lone ;
  The night winds were sighing around his abode
    'Mong the trees of the forest with eeriest moan.
His face was deep furrowed with many a year,
  But his eye, like the eagle's, was piercing and keen ;
And his hair, thickly matted in ringlets of grey,
  Hung o'er his thin shoulders in silvery sheen.

Thus he lived all alone, in seclusion from men,
  And was feared as a wizard the country around ;
From his hut those astray on the wide moor at night
  Often heard in wild music the harp's measure
    sound.
Its note was the wail of a sorrowing heart
  That in life's sunny morn was lightsome and glad,
K

When the now withered hermit had mixed with the
  crowd,
And his figure so manly with beauty was clad.

Ah ! yes, down the vista of years he could see
  The time when ambition his bosom had fired ;
When his clansmen around him in plaided array
  For battle were marshalled, with valour inspired ;
When the cry of " Prince Charlie " made claymores
  flash bare,
  As they circled their young chief so gallant and
    brave ;
But his hopes, fondly cherished, were crushed in the
  bloom
  When the flower of the North made Culloden their
    grave.

Then, outlawed and hunted, he fled to the wilds,
  Where beasts of the forest securely may roam ;
The house of his fathers to flame given over,
  The chieftain was left neither shelter nor home.
He loved with devotion the land of his sires ;
  A hut on its moors, 'mid the heather's wild bloom,
Was dearer to him than a home o'er the ocean—
  Thus lived he alone in seclusion and gloom.

—◇—

My Home.

O my home in the north, far away 'mong the hills,
  My memory oft lovingly strays,
And my bosom with sweetest emotion aye fills
  When I think of the heath-covered braes.

Though o'er the skies darkly the clouds may career,
  And the mountains stand rugged and bare,

No land of the sun to my heart is so dear,
   For the home of my childhood is there.

No pleasures that gladden the heart can I find
   Like the pleasures of youth's happy day ;
And with mem'ries of love in my bosom enshrined
   Is my home in the north far away.

—◇—

Earlston.

THE banks and braes of Earlston,
   So lovely to be seen
      When clad in Spring with beauteous flowers,
   And wild woods waving green.
The birds carol by Carolside
   Through all the sunny hours,
And amorous lovers hand in hand
   Stray 'mid the vernal bowers.
The martial legions of old Rome,
   They rested here awhile,
Encamped on yonder sable hill
   To bask in Nature's smile.
To wander by thy limpid streams,
   And revel in thy charms
Forgetting mid the raptured scenes
   The curse of war's alarms.
And Cowden knowes, though greater bards
   Have sung thy praises well,
I'll strike my lyre and join their choir
   The chorus loud to swell.
I've seen the morning sun adorn
   The hills with golden light,
And twilight shadows falling dim
   Bespeak the dewy night.

I've roved mid scenes by Nature blist
    With beauties rich and rare,
But few with thine, sweet Earlston,
    Could ever I compare.

—◇—

Bonnie Banff.

O! BONNIE BANFF! where waters meet
    'Tween leafy wood and flowing wave,
    You proudly stand, while round your feet
The rushing tides of Deveron lave.
When early spring, with bursting buds,
    Wakes all the warbling feathered throng,
Amid Montcoffer's greening woods
    They sing their first and sweetest song.
And there, when summer's flowery wreath
    Hangs fresh and fair on every bough,
The youthful lovers' hearts out-breathe
    The old and oft-repeated vow.
Around them smiling Nature sings,
    Her wanton song with joy they list;
Each merry note that gladsome rings
    Finds echo in each throbbing breast.
And landward if they may not rove,
    O! bonnie Banff! they have thy bay,
Where they may row and whisper love
    Amid the music of the spray.
O! bonnie Banff! where waters meet
    'Tween leafy wood and flowing wave,
You proudly stand while round your feet
    The rushing tides of Deveron lave.

—◇—

Alvah.

WHEN the wild woods of Alvah are waving in
  green,
  And the birds are carolling their love notes so
  free,
When the braes in their mantle of flowerets are seen
And the clover's sweet blossom adorns the lea.

'Tis pleasant to wander among the green dells,
  And see by the streamlets the wild roses fair,
While on the wide moorland the bonnie blue bells
  Are nodding their plumes in the soft summer air.

'Twas by this sweet spot that in life's rosy morn
  So freely I wandered with heart light and gay,
The pleasures of youth did my pathway adorn
  And shadows of care never darkened my way.

How oft when oppressed by the troubles and sorrow
  Which circle us round in this valley of tears,
We're cheered by a gleam of the sunshine we borrow
  From memories and pleasures of earlier years.

The Majesty of Law.

It will be remembered that not long ago the attention of the public
was called to a mean case, which took place in an English jail, through
indignant newspaper paragraphs commenting on the low officialism that
deliberately ordered a poor tame mouse to be killed as it afforded some
degree of pleasure to a prisoner.

WHEN Justice with unerring hands
  Binds on the prisoners' iron bands,
    And seals the wretch's doom,
Within his lonely prison cell
No kindly friend may e'er he hail
  To cheer his hours of gloom.

His soul, unseared by deepest crimes,
Despairing broods o'er happier times,
  Ere dark Temptation came
With serpent stealth his life to blight,
And settled down like starless night
  Enshrouding his fair name.

While pondering thus, his hollow eye
Faint in the corner doth descry
  A sportive mousie play.
This humble creature of the dust,
He tames it, feeds it from his crust,
  And whiles dull time away.

To watch its sprightly little ways,
As gaily round his feet it plays
  All innocence and glee;
He learns to love his little mate,
That shares with him a wretch's fate
  'Mid gloom and misery.

But brutal jailers note the pair,
And with official frowns they swear—
  Those senseless, brainless fools,
That pleasure thus, though void of harm,
Might lend to prison life a charm,
  Which is against the rules.

Those human brutes, to cruelty drilled,
The inoffensive mouse they killed
  With stern severity!
Such act would shame a heathen Turk,
Yet this was British jailers' work,
  And Law's high Majesty!

The Lament.

AROUND me, with a whispered song,
  The summer zephyrs blow,
    And fragrance sweet of flow'rets fair
    By bank and stream that grow.

O'erhead the skies are azure blue,
  The wild woods robed in green,
With singing birds on every spray,
  Adorns the raptured scene.

The river pours its crystal floods
  Along its verdant shore,
While Nature smiles on every side,
  My anguished heart is sore.

I come to this sequestered nook
  To breathe my bitter woe;
'Twas here we made our parting vow
  But one short year ago.

But cruel Death has snatched the prize
  I set my heart upon;
With sorrow now I hold my tryst,
  And wander here alone.

—◇—

Human Life.

AS rivers down the vale of earth
  Flow onward to the sea,
    So man glides down the vale of time
    On to eternity,
Amid whose dim uncertain light,
Like phantom 'mid the shades of night,
He vanishes from mortal sight,
And all he leaves behind of life
  Is a fading memory.

A Sad Incident.

THE setting sun, all rosy red,
    'Mid clouds of gold and grey
  Was slowly sinking, while the shade
    That curtains night from day
Drew slowly o'er the eastern hills,
    And clad the vales in gloom,
And misty vapours from the rills
    Bedewed the flowers in bloom.

'Twas in this witching evening hour,
    Deep in a rural glade,
A swain enamoured sought the bower
    Which held his darling maid.
He spied her in a dusky nook,
    And with extended arms,
While all his frame with pleasure shook,
    He rushed to drink her charms.

He clasped her fondly to his breast
    In love's wild ardent dream,
But when her lips he sought to taste
    She gave a fearful scream.
And wildly fled, all streaming faced,
    To hide her horrid woes,
The eager fool in raptured haste—
    Had bit the darling's nose.

—◇—

I Love.

I LOVE the real, the rosy kiss,
    I love no kiss of fancy;
  I love the love that yields the bliss
    Of Venus' necromancy.

I love to speak my love in words,
    And when these fail, in glances;
I hate all false, æsthetic birds
    With plumage of romances.

The little brook, with merry glee,
    From out its sunny waters,
With voice and words of melody
    Sings unto Flora's daughters.
The little birds, to nature true,
    Each unto each pipes cheery,
And so my lips shall speak to you,
    My bonnie, winsome dearie.

The nightingale at evening sings,
    The lark at rosy morning,
And all the world of nature rings,
    " Æsthetic silence " scorning.
I love to hear the maiden laugh,
    I love to see her dancing—
These are the corn of life—the chaff
    Is dull æsthete's romancing.

——◇——

Willie's Adieu.

YOU go to leave us, Willie, lad,
    But only for a while ;
Your presence aye could make us glad,
    And weary care beguile.

And oft again we'll wish you back
    To join our jovial corps,
And with your ever social talk
    To cheer us as of yore.

May northern air, so fresh and free,
    Restore your faded bloom,

And bring the lustre to your e'e
That's fled 'mid Glasgow's gloom.

The darling lassie that you lo'e,
  Once more within your arms,
Will happiness and strength renew
  .By all her artless charms.

A potent spell is love, indeed,
  To chase away our ills ;
By it the streams of bliss are freed,
  And gush like summer rills

That, bound in ice, so chilly lay
  Till by the sunbeams strong
Released, they gaily gushed away
  To ripple merry song.

Then though you leave us, Willie, man,
  'Tis only for a time ;
Remember this whene'er you scan
  This little farewell rhyme.

The North Countrie.

THERE'S valour and worth in the north countrie,
    Freedom had its birth in the north countrie ;
  For the Roman soldiers' lot was to perish and to
    rot
    'Mong the wilds and the wastes of the north
    countrie.

England came with brag to the north countrie,
  With bluster and brag to the north countrie ;

But she learned to her cost that no power of mortal
   host
Could crush the gallant hearts of the north countrie.

The hearts all are warm in the north countrie,
   And life has a charm in the north countrie;
For the lads are brave and braw, and the lasses
   loving a'
That live among the hills of the north countrie.

Up among the hills of the north countrie,
   'Mong the hills and the dells of the north countrie,
The hardy thistle blows, and the purple heather
   grows
Sae bonnie 'mong the snows of the north countrie.

Stormy skies grow clear in the north countrie
   When spring decks the year in the north countrie;
Then the little birdies sing, till the hills and valleys
   ring
With music sweet and fine in the north countrie.

Then, ho! for the hearts of the north countrie,
   The homes and the hearts of the north countrie;
While valour and true worth have a place upon the
   earth
They'll flourish 'mong the hills of the north countrie.

—◆—

Bonnie Blue-E'ed Annie.

THE Bard o' Coila sang o' Jean,
   An' mony a sweet an' winsome quean,
But I will only sing o' ane—
   My bonnie, blue-e'ed Annie.

The flower o' womankin' is she;
Her happy smile an' laugh sae free
Are mair than stores o' gowd to me—
    My bonnie, blue-e'ed Annie.

Nae wile nor guile can hae a part
Within her tender truthfu' heart;
My lassie's free fae ilka art—
    My bonnie, blue-e'ed Annie.

E'en, thinkin' o' my lassie's charms,
The circlin' tide within me warms;
Oh! were she but within my arms—
    My bonnie, blue-e'ed Annie.

Her voice is like a melody,
That ever cheers an' gladdens me;
Light on my life, pride o' my e'e—
    My bonnie, blue-e'ed Annie.

Ye Powers on High, I crave ae boon,
Mair dear to me than monarch's croon,
Grant it to me, an' grant it soon—
    My bonnie, blue-e'ed Annie.

Dear Blue Eyes.

DEAR blue eyes, that beam for me
    Like stars in yonder night,
  O, dear blue eyes, you seem to me
    Like gems of azure light.
O, dear blue eyes, O, dear blue eyes,
  When dreams of youth depart,
And every flower of fancy dies
  You still will cheer my heart.
    O, dear blue eyes.

O, dear blue eyes, I seem to see
 Within your light so fair
The gates on high " ajar for me,"
 And angels waiting there.
O, dear blue eyes, O, dear blue eyes,
 For ever kind and clear,
A world of love within you lies,
 And truth for ever dear.
 O, dear blue eyes.

O, dear blue eyes, when stars shall live
 No more to light the night,
O, dear blue eyes, you then shall give
 A purer, brighter light.
O, dear blue eyes, O, dear blue eyes,
 For ever kind and clear,
I'll hail you then beyond the skies
 The brightest of that sphere.

—◇—

The Brave Old Thistle.

THE brave old thistle still flourishes free
 In the brave old land that's girt by the sea,
 The emblem of Scotland and libertie!
 The brave old thistle, the thistle, hurrah!
Chorus.—Hurrah, for the thistle, the grand old thistle,
 Proudly it waves when the wild storms
 whistle,
 Tossing its plume on the gales of the
 mountains—
 The thistle of Scotland for ever, hurrah!

Bright is its crest in the glory of flower,
Decking our valleys and mountains that tower,

Emblem of Scotland, of freedom and power—
   The brave old thistle, the thistle, hurrah !
      Hurrah, for the thistle, &c.

He that hath handled it rudely well knows
The sting that a Scot presents to his foes ;
Press it the harder and fiercer it grows—
   The brave old thistle, the thistle, hurrah !
      Hurrah, for the thistle, &c.

Under its thorn is a bosom of down,
Tender and soft though 'tis hid by a frown ;
Nature has stamped it a king with a crown—
   The brave old thistle, the thistle, hurrah !
      Hurrah, for the thistle, &c.

Fair is the rose of old England to see,
And dear is the shamrock, O ! Erin, to thee,
But fearless we boast the lord of the three—
   The brave old thistle, the thistle, hurrah !
      Hurrah, for the thistle.

—◇—

How Fair in the Dawning.

NOW fair in the dawning spring-time
   Is the bud upon the tree,
  And sweet in the dawning spring-time
    Is the song bird's melodie ;
But sweet as the young bud tender,
  And fairer far to see,
Is the form of my love so slender,
  With the love-light in her e'e.

No song that a bird can render,
  As it pipes full merrilie,

Is half so sweet and so tender
  As the voice of my love to me.
Then sing, ye birds of the spring-time,
  In a clear and joyous lay,
While I with my love shall wander
  In the gloamin' blythe and gay.

O my heart is ever gladsome,
  For spring is aye with me,
And flowers in my heart are blooming
  In beauty constantly.
As I wander with my dearie
  All things seem fair to see;
E'en the smoke-clouds play like sun beams
  As they drift o'er her and me.

—◇—

The Emigrants' Song.

UPON the deck we sit, as fast
  The vessel speeds along,
    And sing in chorus with the blast
Our sad and farewell song.

Farewell, farewell, our childhood's home,
  Adieu, our native land,
Far, far from thee we go to roam
  Upon a foreign strand.

Adieu, adieu, our dearest friends,
  And fast receding shore,
A voice re-echoes in the winds
  We'll never see you more.

Farewell, old Scotia's heathy hills,
  And all her smiling vales,

Each eye with sorrow's fountain fills,
    As fill the swelling sails.

Cursed be the tyrant powers that drive
    Us from our lowly home,
While game may freely live and thrive,
    Why have we thus to roam?

We leave the dearest land on earth,
    Where kindred dust is laid,
And blackened ruins mark the hearth
    Where joyously we played.

Oh, shades of night, close thick and dark,
    And howl, ye stormy waves,
Around our swiftly-speeding barque
    'Mid ocean's foamy caves.

The cloudy night grows black above,
    And all around is drear,
As fast we leave the land we love,
    And all our hearts hold dear.

And drear and sad are they that sing
    This farewell song to thee,
While speeding on the tempest's wing
    Far o'er the heaving sea.

—◇—

'Mong Yonder Knowes.

[AIR—"Gae bring to me a pint o' wine."

'MONG yonder knowes a burnie rows,
    An' siller sauchs grow lang an' bonnie,
    'Twas there yestreen at edge o' e'en
I met my ain, my darlin' Johnny.

He is a braw an' bythesome lad,
  An' weel I wat a brave an' bonnie,
There's nae a lad in a' the shire
  That I wad hae afore my Johnny.

O' warld's gear though he be scant
  He has twa han's, can work wi' ony,
I'd tak' my chance an' never fear
  For want as laug's I had my Johnny.

Wad he but seek my han' the nicht,
  An' wile me oot amang the mony,
Sae blythe an' ready 's I wad gang
  An' happy live wi' my ain Johnny.

War-Song of Erin.

O! WHEN will the day-star of Erin arise,
  O! when will the gloom of her night dis-
    appear,
Say when will the bright streak illumine her skies
That heralds the day of her liberty near?

Must bigotry trample on right yet awhile,
  And tread down her children as slaves in the mire,
Will justice long trammelled upon them smile?
  Yes crushed, but not dead, is their manhood and
    fire.

Arise queenly Erin, arise in thy might,
  And summon thy sons to thy green Island shore,
One grand inspiration shall nerve them to fight,—
  'Tis the wrongs of their fathers and memorios of
    yore.

L

United and true to themselves and their cause,
  Obeying one leader and owning one law;
Uplift the Green Flag, and the breeze as it blows
  Shall swell the loud war-cry of Erin-go-Bragh.

Thy valourous sons in their thousands shall come
  To swell thy battalions, and chargers shall wheel
At the blast of thy bugle and roll of thy drum,
  While bayonets glitter like forests of steel.

Arise then, O! Erin, and strike now the blow
  And stand 'fore the world in majesty free,
Then Liberty's dawn o'er thy hill tops shall glow,
  And crown thee with glory, bright gem of the sea.

My Heart's Delight.

AIR.—*Finnigan's Wake.*

! IRISH lasses, Irish glasses,
    Shure, they are my hearts delight,
  'Tis no matter where I wander
  Follow me their faces bright.

O! the darlin's, how I love them,
  But they are the jewels nate,
Wake or sleep they are my pleasure,
  Better far than butcher mate.

There's Biddy now, the darlin' cratur's
  Played the divel with my heart,
By St Patrick! if she leaves me
  Soul and body shure will part.

I've got myself a little cabin,
  And bedad! no rint I'll pay—

If the landlord comes to bother,
Troth, 'twill be his dyin' day.

Like a shamrock shure I'll flourish
With my pigs and Biddy dear,
And my rifle o'er the chimney,
Faith! no evil will I fear.

---⋄---

The Corn-Spirit's Song.

S 'mid the fields to-day I stand,
The rustling corn about me sighing,
Its thousand voices low and grand
Seem music of the years undying.
I hear the spirit of the grain
Piping the golden reeds among;
And as I list the mystic strain
Methinks I read its wordless song :

A thousand thousand summer suns
Have glinted on my leaf;
A thousand thousand autumns brown
Have kissed me in the sheaf.
Since the blue days of early time
The merry reapers' song
I've listened to in every clime
My harvest sheaves among.
I've seen the lovers' sparkling eyes,
And felt their warm breath,
As 'mong the corn they knit the ties
That stretch thro' life and death.
And downward thro' the rolling years,
Beneath each autumn sun,
I hear that tale of joy and tears,
For life is never done;

And races come and races go,
  As harvests rise and wane,
But youthful hearts forever glow,
  And come to reap the grain.
New faces 'mong the rigs I see,
  And voices new 1 hear ;
To-day they swing the sickle free,
  But soon they'll disappear.
And I in other years shall see
  A race to-day unborn
Come, merry-hearted, joyously,
  To gather in the corn ;
For I, the spirit of the grain,
  Shall pipe the reeds among,
While harvest moons shall rise and wane,
  Or heard is reapers' song.

Dreams.

YOUTH dreams of the future, and age of the past,
    And sweet are the dreams of to-day while they
      last ;
But dearest are dreams of old hearts beating slow—
  They borrow their charms from long, long ago.
Chorus.—Long, long ago, long, long ago,
      Dear are the dreams of the long, long ago.

Faces and forms flit around us for ever,
  And memories long buried come back with a glow ;
Like swallows of summer they hover and quiver,
  Those gladsome old mem'ries of long, long ago.
        Long, long ago, &c.

Bright were the skies of those far away summers,
  And fairer the flowers seemed to blossom and grow ;

So welcome forever those silent-winged comers,
 The dreams and the mem'ries of long, long ago.
  Long, long ago, &c.

O! drink of the goblet of youth as it reams,
 For age comes a-pace with its furrows and snow;
But happy's the heart that's filled with the dreams,
 The faces, and fancies of long, long ago.
  Long, long ago, &c.

—◇—

The Fame of "Tam o' Shanter."

(Suggested by the great popularity of Tam's cap with both sexes.)

FAME is but a fleeting thing,
 And passes at a canter;
All but the fame of him I sing—
 Immortal "Tam o' Shanter."

Since first the glory of his name
 Illumined Burns' pages,
The light of his undying fame
 Has shone adown the ages.

The sweetest maids upon their heads
 Wear "Tam o' Shanter" bonnets,
Bedecked with varying hued cockades
 All worthy of our sonnets;

And gentlemen of all degrees,
 If they would be enchanters
Of ladies fair, must never cease .
 To don their "Tam o' Shanters."

The Bard o' Coila's" name may fade,
 And people ne'er think on it,

Before their heads they cease to shade
  With "Tam o' Shanter's" bonnet.

The greatest worthies Burns sung,
  Wi' a' his merry banter,
Completely in the shade are flung,
  Compared wi' "Tam o' Shanter."

But while we Tammas thus revere,
  Do not forget his crony;
In *leather aprons* all appear,
  And honour "Souter Johnny."

Fame is indeed a fleeting thing,
  And passes at a canter;
But for eternity shall ring
  The fame of "Tam o' Shanter."

—◇—

Ever Thinking.

EVER thinking of thee, darling,
  Ever thinking all the day,
    And by night in dreams thy vision
    O'er my spirit holds the sway.

I can see thy bright eyes beaming
  Full of tender love to me,
And in fancy hear thee murmur
  Words of sweetest melody.

And my soul is filled with rapture
  When I think upon that love
Warm and tender—an affection
  Pure as angels feel above.

O! my lips can never weary
  Of repeating my heart's song—

The undying love I'll bear thee
Through eternity so long.

For when life hath ceased, my darling,
I shall not have told the sum
Of my spirit's deep devotion,
But the after-time shall come.

And in that long day of glory
I shall gaze upon thy brow,
And shall tell to thee, my darling,
All the love I cannot now.

Through the cycles never ending
I shall view thy spirit fair;
But, O! heaven would not be heaven,
Love, to me without thee there.

Every mark of sweet affection
That thou doest bestow on me,
Fans to warmer heat the feeling
Of my quenchless love for thee.

Let our souls unite for ever,
Let them never severed be,
But as one to live together
Through the long eternity.

---◇---

I Wove My Love a Garland.

I WOVE my love a garland fair,
   And twined it in her bonnie hair
That hung in wavy ringlets rare
      Aboot her neck sac slender;
An' straying 'mang the woodland bowers,
We poo'd the sweetest summer flowers,

All heedless o' the passin' hours,
Beguiled wi' love sae tender.

We watched the sportive butterfly
On gaudy wing gae flittin' by,
As slowly faded frae the sky
    The sunset's gowden splendour.
The dusky shades o' gloamin' fell,
An' o'er us threw their witchin' spell,
As slowly doon the pensive dell
    We han' in han' did wander.

An' underneath a wild rose tree
We sat us doon, my love an' me,
To list the sweetest melody
    That Nature's voice can render.
Upon a wavin' flowery spray
A linnet sang its evenin' lay
To serenade the closin' day
    In notes baith wild an' tender.

I drew my lassie to my breast,
Syne put my arm aboot her waist,
Sae fond her dewy lips to taste,
    An' me she didna hinder;
An' underneath the wild rose tree
We vowed as ane to live an' dee,
Wi' hearts o' love an' constancy
    That nane should ever sunder.

—◇—

Ann of Aberdeen.

OF all the maidens young and fair
    And graceful I have seen,
    There's none for beauty can compare
With Ann of Aberdeen.

A witching light dwells in her eye,
　Her step is light and free ;
Her blooming cheeks the rose outvie
　Which springs by bonnie Dee.
Her artless charms have won my heart,
　She reigns my bosom queen ;
No power to me can joy impart
　Like Ann of Aberdeen.
And when between my love and me
　There stretches many a mile,
In fondest fancy oft I see
　Her form, and mark her smile.
Her vision comes to cheer my heart,
　As dews refresh the flower ;
Her fancied smile can bliss impart,
　And gladden many an hour.
Where is the maiden young and fair
　Can shoot Love's arrows keen
With aim so sure, and grace so rare,
　As Ann of Aberdeen ?

—◇—

A Psalm-Song.

GRANT, guid Lord, thy ain blessing fair
　On the lassie o' my love ;
May the gems o' grace shine roon' her rare,
　Like the licht o' stars above.

I love her, Lord, with a strong heart's love
　That hath room for nought but she—
But she. an' the guid, kind Lord above
　That hath granted her to me.

O ! were I in heaven high this nicht
　I'd lie on its starry floor,

And look through the sheen o' heaven's licht
On the lassie I adore.

Heaven's sangs would hae nae music sweet
Till I heard my lassie's voice,
An' the splendours o' the gowden street
Wadna mak' my heart rejoice.

I'd watch an' wait till she cam' to me
Through the hours baith ear' an' late,
An' first o' the throng sae joyfully
I would meet her at heav'n's gate.

O! grant to her, Lord, the croon o' peace,
May her life frae woe be free,
And blessing her, Lord, Thou wilt increase
The joy thou hast gi'en to me.

—◇—

Love's Fond Kiss.

WHAT a world of raptured bliss
Dwells in love's fond, ardent kiss;
Glowing warm, the soul's emotion
Surges like the waves of ocean.

Twined in young affection's arms,
Lost in maze of sweetest charms;
O! the bliss, the joy, the woe,
That from love's fond kiss doth flow.

—◇—

The Far Countrie.

BEYOND this mortal sphere lies a far countrie,
Each weary pilgrim here hies to that countrie,

Where all is bright and fair, for no sorrow enters
  there—
They're free from toil and care in that far countrie.

The groves with music ring in that far countrie,
There reigns eternal spring in that far countrie;
The flowers for ever blow, and the breezes whisper
  low,
As they wander to and fro in that far countrie.

The skies are ever clear in that far countrie,
The days are never drear in that far countrie ;
The fountains flowing bright ever sparkle in the
  light
That never wanes to night in that far countrie.

The bowers are ever green in that far countrie,
No chilly winter keen comes to that countrie ;
The treasures of our heart from earth when they de-
  part
Are free from trouble's dart in that far countrie.

Loving friends will greet us in that far countrie,
Joy and love will meet us in that far countrie ;
Earth's jealousies nor hate can enter at the gate
To mar the happy state of that far countrie.

The stream of life is flowing to that far countrie,
Our friends are ever going to that far countrie ;
The weary are at rest in that home of the blest,
And the ruling king is Christ in that far countrie.

The Yule Log.

COME stir ye up the Yule-log, friends,
　　Until the chimney roar,
　　Just as the good folks used to do
　　　On Christmas nights of yore,
And sit ye round the ample hearth,
　　And in its cheerful glow
I'll tell you of a Christmas-time—
　　A Christmas long ago.

The snow is deep, and cold to-night,
　　The frosty stars gleam clear,
And shine upon the world, my friends,
　　As they've done many a year.
But many a year has come and gone
　　With many a winter's snow,
And many a blazing Yule-log since
　　That Christmas long ago.

Nigh nineteen centuries have fled
　　Since Christian hope had birth—
Since the Child in Bethlehem's manger
　　Was born to bless the earth—
Since the host of heavenly angels
　　Sang peace to earth below,
And the hearts of men were gladdened
　　That Christmas long ago.

They sang good-will and peace on earth,
　　The shepherds heard the strain
While watching on that Christmas night
　　Their flocks on Bethlehem's plain.
Nigh nineteen hundred years have fled,
　　But still by high and low
Remembered is that Christmas time—
　　That Christmas long ago.

Pile high the board with social cheer,
    Brown ale and smoking roast,
And let good-will and fellowship
    Be our especial toast;
For on this night through all the years
    The blazing Yule-log's glow
Has cheered the hearths and hearts of men
    Since Christmas long ago.   .

Let jovial plenty be our toast,
    And temperance hold the rein,
Lest from our hearts excess should blot
    True joy, and leave a stain;
And as we stir the Christmas fire
    To make the Yule-log glow,
Remember Him who blessed the earth
    That Christmas long ago.

—◇—

Merry Jamie Ritchie.

A' the chiels that e'er I saw
    Wha could wi' fun bewitch ye,
    He shines a king ootowre them a'—
Does merry Jamie Ritchie.
Chorus.—O! merry Jamie Ritchie,
    O! jolly Jamie Ritchie,
    The blithest chiel that e'er I saw
Is merry Jamie Ritchie.

When press't wi' care, as aft you'll be,
    An' life seems dull an' weary,
Just doon to Ibrox gang and see
    The chiel that's ever cheery.
    O! merry, &c.

He'll sing you sangs, an' stories tell
 Aboot his pranks in India ;
O' rovin' life he's had a spell,
 An' guid advice can lend ye,
  O ! merry, &c.

He's got a han'some, clever wife
 Wha helps him to bewitch ye,
An' solid sense wi' her is rife,
 As fun wi' Jamie Ritchie.
  O ! merry, &c.

He likes fu' weel a social glass,
 " The wheels o' life it greases,"
So Burns sang, wha wis nae ass,
 An' Scotland braid he pleases.
  O ! merry, &c.

Noo let us wish their healths combined,—
 His ain an' his guid lady's,
An' heartily recall to mind
 Hoo happy aft they made us.
  O ! merry, &c.

Love's Doubt—A Duet.

SHE.

THOUGH the flower of youth around me weaves
 All its tendrils sweet to-day,
 Will you love me 'mid the falling leaves
As amid the blooms of May ?

When my cheek hath lost its rosy hue,
 And my tresses dark grow grey,
Shall I still remain as dear to you
 As amid the blooms of May ?

When my lips have lost their luscious charm,
  And my eyes their light so gay,
Will you shield me with your loving arm
  As fond as you do to-day?

HE.

My darling, you will be dear to me
  When your hair, now dark, is grey,
And your form hath lost the witchery
  Of sweet youth's bright early day ;

Though your cheek may lose its rosy hue,
  And your eyes their lustre gay,
O! my love will still be strong for you
  As amid the blooms of May.

For I too, my love, must sink and wane,
  And my vigour fade away,
But our hearts shall still the same remain
  As amid the blooms of May.

Our love shall grow in the after years
  Still stronger with time, I say,
Then banish for aye the doubts and fears,
  My love, that you feel to-day.

For in my heart sweet affection breathes
  A song I shall echo alway—
'Tis, " I'll love you 'mid the falling leaves
  As amid the blooms of May."

—◇—

My Soldier Lad.

AIR.—*John Highlandman.*

HEN war's alarms all were past,
  And bugles sang no rousing blast

To bid the charging squadrons close,
And gleaming steel to steel oppose,

The gallant soldiers homeward came
Bedecked with wreaths of martial fame,
Their blazoned standards, rent and torn,
O'er many a desperate field were borne.

Where'er they waved the combat grew—
The showers of laden bullets flew,
And 'neath their folds the gallant brave
Aye victory won, or glory's grave.

These scenes of blood are now all o'er,
The echoes of the cannon's roar
Resound not o'er th' embattled plains,
Where fell the showers of crimson rains.

And now my love is safe at home,
No more again will e'er he roam,
Or leave me all alone to mourn
And sigh in grief for his return.

What though those scars be on his cheek,
It is not beauty that I seek ;
Those marks of honour I behold
With pride upon my soldier bold.

Love's Melody.

SLOW, blow, ye summer zephyrs, blow
Across the honey scented lea,
A song of love is in your breath
Of breezy melody to me.

Blow, blow ye summer zephyrs, blow
  And stir the leaves on every tree,
Their rustling sound is music sweet—
  A melody of love to me.

Blow, blow ye summer zephyrs, blow
  And stir the waves on every sea,
There's music in their hollow roar—
  A melody of love to me.

Blow, blow ye summer zephyrs, blow,
  And stir the maiden's tresses fair,
And softly kiss her ruby lip—
  A melody of love is there.

Blow, blow ye summer zephyrs, blow,
  And stir the roses on yon tree,
Their tapping on the window pane
  Is love's sweet melody to me.

Blow, blow ye summer zephyrs, blow
  Around the bower in yonder grove,
My love is there, blow soft, and sing
  To her your melody of love.

—◇—

The Burn.

A DOWN sweet Rosieburn's howe,
  'Tween banks where rush and brackens grow,
So clear yon burnie's waters flow,
  Like silver to the sea.
Chorus.—O, let me hear its song again,
  As, dashing on to join the main,
It chants the same unwearied strain
  In youth it sang to me.

M

Oft have I wandered by its stream,
When summer sunlight there did gleam,
To o'er the future fondly dream,
    With heart so light and free.
      O, let me hear its song again, &c.

And in its murmur soft and low
Sweet voices in the long ago
Spoke from the rippling waters' flow
    Bright words of hope to me.
      O, let me hear its song again, &c,

How oft my fancy takes the wing
To hear again the birdies sing,
Where flowers of Rosieburn spring
    In beauty wild and free.
      O, let me hear its song again, &c.

It cheers my heart when far away,
Where bustling commerce holds the sway,
To ponder, 'mid the daily fray,
    On rustic scenes I lo'e.
      O, let me hear its song again, &c.

Amid life's war of right and wrong,
Ah! oft my wearied heart doth long
To hear the rippling burnie's song
    It murmured long ago.
    O, let me hear its song again, &c.

—◇—

London Scots.

TUNE.—*A' the airts the win' can blaw.*

YE London Scots, your voices raise
    To swell this homely strain,
An' bring to mind the bonnie braes
    O' Scotland ance again.

Forget a while the restless stream
  O' London's weary sea,
And hie us home where torrents gleam
  'Mong Scotland's mountains free.

Though round us London's mighty domes,
  An' London's splendours shine,
We ne'er forget oor northern homes,
  And scenes o' "Auld Lang Syne."
We mingle with a stranger race,
  An' stranger tongues we hear;
Yet ne'er forget or lo'e we less
  Oor native Doric dear.

The sturdy language o' oor sires
  Oor hearts it aye can warm ;
Its tone o' manly vigour fires,
  Or melts wi' simple charm.
It brings us back the early days
  O' sunny youth an' home,
When, sportin' lightsome o'er the braes,
  We had nae thochts to roam.

Sae haud in hand, like brither Scots,
  Wi' siccar grip an' true,
Whate'er in life oor various lots,
  We'll pledge the land we lo'e.
Then, London Scots, your voices raise
  In Caledonian strain,
An' bring to mind the bonnie braes
  O' Scotland ance again.

Thy Gallant Hearts, Britannia.

THY gallant hearts, Britannia,
  Are trusty, brave, and true ;
Thy gallant hearts, Britannia,
  Like them there are but few.
Thy sons and beauteous daughters
  Are famed the world wide ;
And ocean's rolling waters
  They lave thy shores in pride.
Chorus.—O ! thy maiden hearts, Britannia,
    How kind in love are they ;
    And thy manly hearts, Britannia,
    Are fearless in the fray.

And may thy hearts, Britannia,
  Be ever this, say we,
To guard thee, O ! Britannia,
  The noble and the free.
May love and happiness remain
  To cheer each cosy home,
And welcome back thy sons again
  That distant from thee roam.
Chorus.—O ! thy maiden hearts, Britannia,
    How kind in love are they ;
    And thy manly hearts, Britannia,
    Are fearless in the fray.

The War o' Life.

VAIN human life is but a strife
  Where we maun tak' a part,
An' weary fight for weary life,
  Sair galled by mony a dart.

Chorus.—But never try to flee the field,
  Or shun the honest war, man;
  Success is his wha disna yield,
  An' honoured is ilk scar, man.

An' some hae aye to gruesome fight,
  Wi' constant foes oppress't;
While they in siller armour bright
  Hae aften time to rest.
    But never try to flee, &c.

Grim carle, care, wi' empty pouch,
  Is aft oor sairest foe;
An' woe to them wha face the slouch
  Wi' nought to fend his blow.
    But never try to flee, &c.

Some silly chiels hae tried the drink
  When they had him to meet,
An' left, on cauldrif ruin's brink,
  Their wives an' bairns to greet.
    But never try to flee, &c.

Some, swaggerin' wi' a dizzy brain,
  An' belly rumblin' teem,
Hae thocht that care an' want were slain,
  But found it was a dream.
    Sae never try to flee, &c.

A sturdy will an' steady han',
  Wi' heart o' sterlin' ring,
Are weapons that will tak' the van,
  An' a' your foes owrefling.
    But never try to flee, &c.

—◇—

My Dearie, O.

FAIR is the earth when flowers in May
    Are springin' sweet an' bonnie, O;
But her I lo'e, sae blythe an' gay,
    Is sweeter far than ony, O.
Chorus.—Sweeter far than ony, O,
        There's nae a flower sae bonnie, O,
        That springs in garden, cot, or ha'
        As my ain artless dearie, O.

She's graceful as the sportive fawn,
    When tripping light an' airy, O ;
She scarce disturbs the dewy lawn,
    My heart-beguiling fairy, O.
        Sweeter far than ony, O, &c.

Her lip is like the budding rose,
    She's tender, sweet, an' coy, O ;
Her cheek sae soft, like peach it glows,
    My love and lasting joy, O.
        Sweeter far than ony, O, &c.

Her witchin' een they glowin' glance,
    With lights o' love a-beamin', O ;
An' when in glee they brightly dance,
    Like orient stars a-gleamin', O.
        Sweeter far than ony, O, &c.

Give me my lassie in my arms,
    I seek nae greater blisses, O,
An' I'll repay her maiden charms
    With ardent manly kisses. O.
        Sweeter far than ony, O, &c.

The round o' life would weary be,
    An' earth itsel' seem dreary, O ;

But thoughts o' her sao dear to me
Can keep me bright an' cheery, O.
Sweeter far than ony, O, &c.

---◇---

Our Volunteer Review.

(A New Song to an Old Tune.)

The Scottish Volunteers were reviewed by Her Majesty the Queen at
Edinburgh, August 1881.

COME, Scots, fling up your bonnets blue,
    An' gi'e three cheers, an' a' that;
In honour o' oor gran' review,
    Oor volunteers, an' a' that.
Chorus.—For a' that, an' a' that,
    Brave Caledon, an' a' that,
    Can muster men frae hill an' glen
    To her defen', an' a' that.

Some forty thousand men an' more,
    Wi' guns au' swords, an' a' that,
Were there, wha vow to keep oor shore
    Frae foreign hordes, an' a' that.
    For a' that, etc.

The stalwart warriors o' the north—
    Brigades o' Celts, an' a' that,
In thousands crowded south the Forth,
    Wi' trews an' kilts, an' a' that.
    For a' that, etc.

An' sturdy chiels cam' frae the west,
    Sao stout an' strong, an' a' that;
An' frae the borders up they press't,
    A martial throng, an' a' that.
    For a' that, etc.

The gallant '' Scottish '' e'en were there,
　Frae Lunnon toon, an' a' that—
For hame they cam' the *fete* to share,
　Ilk wanderin' loon, an' a' that.
　　　　For a' that, etc.

There's scarce a part o' Scotland wide
　But sent its corps, an' a' that,
To march Edina's streets wi' pride,
　An' pass the Queen, an' a' that.
　　　　For a' that, etc.

An' soldier like, mid mud an' mire,
　They did their pairts, an' a' that,
Wi' drums an' bands to stir an' fire
　Their gallant hearts, an' a' that.
　　　　For a' that, etc.

An' though the Archers wi' their bows
　Looked antique swains, an' a' that,
The proudest blood o' Scotland flows
　Within their veins, an' a' that.
　　　　For a' that, etc.

A body guard to Kings an' Queens,
　When they come here, an' a' that,
Hae been these nobles, an' their frien's
　For mony years, an' a' that.
　　　　For a' that, etc.

Then, Scots, fling up your bonnets blue,
　An' gie three cheers, an' a' that,
In honour o' oor gran' review,
　Oor volunteers, an' a' that.
　　　　For a' that, an' a' that,
　　　　　Brave Caledon, an' a' that,
　　　　Can muster men frae hill and glen
　　　　　To her defen', an' a' that.

A Christmas Morning Wish.

MAY some sweet portion of that heavenly love
   Known by the angels in the realms above
   Be thine, my darling, on this gladsome morn
That He, the Messenger of Love, was born.

And at His throne this day I shall renew
My earnest prayer for happiness to you;
And while I pray for peace and bliss to thee,
O! thrice beloved, do thou remember me.

—◇—

Song.

(FOR LAST NIGHT OF THE YEAR.)

TO the year that is dying come sing an adieu,
   Each moment that's flying brings nearer the
   new;
So let us be merry, my comrades, to-night,
For fresh as the holly our hearts are and light.
Chorus.—O! fresh as the holly
   Our hearts are and jolly,
So let us be merry, my comrades, to-night.

Though time with his wrinkles may furrow our face,
And each hour that tinkles makes shorter our race,
Be merry, my comrades, to-night while we may,
Since sadness nor gladness the moments can stay.
   O! fresh as the holly.

The year that is coming hath pleasures in store,
And sorrows may come as they've often before;
But gaily to-night let us be of good cheer,
And wish for each other a happy New Year.
   O! fresh as the holly.

Then luck to ourselves and the friends of the past,
Good health and good fortune, and long may they
    last;
And fresh as the holly our hearts may they be
Through all the long years that we hope yet to see.
            O! fresh as the holly
            Our hearts are and jolly,
So let us be merry, my comrades, to-night.

—◇—

Do You Remember?

LINES TO A.

O you remember on that autumn day,
    When Alvah's woods in russet glory lay
    Beneath the beams that kissed the ruddy leaves,
    And hastened home the harvest's lingering sheaves?
Do you remember by the bridge we stood,
And gazed far down upon the waveless flood
That dark and sullen thro' the arch did creep,
And formed a lakelet clear and still and deep?
And here together as we voiceless stood,
Where awful calm and solitude did brood,
Where nature's God and nature held the sway,
And all the clanging world seemed far away,
We felt our souls commune, tho' not in words,
And flit together like two mated birds
That fain would rest them 'mid this scene of leaves,
Like weary swallows 'neath the friendly eaves.
Hand clasped in hand, eye centred upon eye,
Each felt that peace and blessedness was nigh ;
Our hearts, long vacant, seemed to glowing feel
Some mighty comfort thro' their portals steal ;
And soft and silvery, like an angel's note,
Low breathe the music of a strain untaught
Of earth, but echoed from that choir above
Whose grandest melody is love, is love.

Aberdeen.

ALL hail! to thee, O Bon-Accord,
    Fair city by the waters,
May thy brave sons their wealth still hoard,
And beauty deck thy daughters.
Thy polished blocks of granite fine
    Are seen in towers ascending,
And to thy streets of graceful line
    Their mirror-lustre lending.
Each noble pile reflects the smile
    Of sunshine brightly gleaming,
With forms that swift or slow do file
    Thy streets in endless streaming.
Great cities of the south uprise,
    In stately form appearing,
'Neath murky, smoke-polluted skies
    That know no summer clearing.
Cloud-kissing stalks of grimy brick,
    The breath of commerce breathing,
Emit their vomit, black and thick,
    In endless fumes upheaving.
And turbid rivers by them glide,
    Whose wavelets ever darkle,
Refuse and filth their tides have dyed,
    That once so pure did sparkle;
But on their bosoms bravely float
    The keels of every nation—
From lands remote those ships have brought
    Us stores of all creation.
And pleasures gay, with every charm,
    Their luring sweets do yield us ;
But ah! they cannot brace the arm
    When manly strength has failed us.
Fair Aberdeen ! thou art the queen
    Of cities great and many,

Undimmed the beauty of thy sheen
　In weather dry or rainy.
Thy granite quarries, far renowned,
　Are sculptors' pride and pleasure,
And round thy brow a wreath they've bound
　Of lasting fame and treasure.
Thy sons are known the world wide
　For prudence, skill, and caution
Where'er their mettle has been tried
　At home or o'er the ocean.
Long flourish, brave old Bon-Accord,
　Fair city by the waters,
And long thy motto, " good accord,"
　Unite thy sons and daughters.

—◇—

The Hill o' Cranna.

TWA miles nor'-east o' Foggyloan
　This hill doth stately rise;
　An' sentry-like the district roon'
　It guards frae a' surprise.

The road that winds around its base
　Its like noo isna kent;
Though nae doot in its early days
　For horse an' cart 'twas meant.

I vow its in an awfu' state,
　Its bottom's fairly gone;
I pity sair the wretch that's late,
　An' comes frae Foggyloan.

The fireflaucht glintin' thro' the moss
　May help to light his way,
But ten to ane he'll wildly toss
　In holes till break o' day.

Oh ! mony a woefu' sicht yon hill
  Has seen in times by-gone,
When staggerin' wi' an extra gill—
  The best in Foggyloan.

Some chiel by nicht wad tak' the road,
  Weel mounted, frae the fair,
An' to the girth beneath its load
  His gallant steed wad lair.

His groans an' cries the hill did mock
  Wi' echoes loud an' sair ;
While man an' beast, as fast as rock,
  Sat siccar planted there,

Till some kind neebors, armed wi' ropes
  An' lamps, came on amain,
An' raised the callan's dying hopes—
  Himsel' an' horse—again.

The Hill o' Cranna bonnie is
  When clad wi' heath in bloom ;
The Hill o' Cranna bonnie is
  When mists do ower it loom.

I've poo'd the berries on its sides
  In days lang past an' gone ;
But clearest in my memory bides
  The road frae Foggyloan.

—◇—

Death of Saul.

(At the battle of Gilboa, with the Philistines.)

GILBOA ! Gilboa ! thy green smiling valley
  Has looked on the grimness of warfare and
  blood,

When Saul and his army to battle did sally
　　Against Philistina's proud valorous flood.
Stately as cedars on Lebanon's mountains,
　　The brave sons of Israel attend the war-call ;
From homes by the hills, by the plains, and the
　　fountains
　　Of Judah, they pour to the banner of Saul.
The shouts of the foemen are drowned in the cheer-
　　ing
　　Of Israel's armies, who rush to the fray,
And their war-steeds and chariots fast are careering
　　In wildly magnificent battle array.
Fierce is the charge, but Saul's army is breaking,
　　And dimmed now with gore is his armour's bright
　　sheen ;
The bows of the heathen his columns are raking
　　With volleys of arrows so galling and keen.
His sons, with the flower of his army, have
　　perished—
　　The pride of his kingdom for ever is gone,
He seeks now for death amongst those that he
　　cherished—
　　Than flee, but to live in dishonour alone.
His bosom is pierced by the shafts swiftly speeding,
　　And strained nigh to breaking is life's slender
　　cord,
And his bearer of armour now listens unheeding
　　As wildly Saul seeks to be pierced by his sword.
He hears the loud shouts of his foemen advancing,
　　And madly he clutches his own bloody brand,
As near him their steel is triumphantly glancing,
　　He falls by his own—not a heathenish hand.
His bearer of armour, who might have gone
　　scathless,
　　Now falls on his blade by the side of the brave ;
Refusing to flee as a minion so faithless,
　　He seeks with his master a glorious grave.

The armies of Judah are broken and flying,
And bitter is Israel's weeping and wail,
For the bravest and best of her children are lying
Like wind-smitten leaves in Gilboa's green vale.

---⧫---

A London Warehouse Sketch.

A WAREHOUSE well and widely known,
Which from a slender stem had grown,
Now daily drives a roaring trade,
Beneath St. Paul's Cathedral shade.

This house at first when only young,
Was all unworthy to be sung,
For trade was scant, and hands were few,
But with the times it grew and grew;

And waxed and swelled till mighty grown,
Its great commercial fame was blown,
O'er all the country far and wide,
It then became a name of pride.

There, maiden beauty reigns supreme,
And faces fair as poets dream,
'Mong Mantles, Feathers, Flowers and Hats,
Shine from the top to basement flats.

And gentlemen of every style,
From they who wear the glossy "tile,"
Down to the men of humble mien,
In scores together there are seen.

But mark, my gentle friends, I pray,
The scenes and faces on some day,
When "Special Shows" have raised the steam,
And briskly flows the trading stream.

The portly Manager in haste,
He shines conspicious o'er the rest,
As business-like he steers the way,
For customers amid the fray.

They first may want to view some shirts,
Of gay design for youthful flirts,
Who angle for a manly prize,
And hope to catch with gaudy flies.

If this be so, then up the stairs
They rush and crush in eager pairs,
And prompt attention to each need,
Ensures a sale with double speed.

Then downward as again they file,
Some tempting "Novelties" beguile,
Parisian bonnets, *a-la-mode*,
Are waiting purchase by the load.

And maidens fair with lily hands
Remove them quickly from the "stands,"
And smile and gush with charming ways,
That fairly Country Buyers daze.

These rustic gents, excited grown,
By City ways to them unknown,
Grimace and stutter as they hop,
'Mong goods "like bulls in china shop."

And 'mong the Feathers, Straws, and Flowers,
Which deck these artificial bowers,
A roaring voice of cadence rare,
Proclaims some great Lieutenant there.

A General, you may bet your hat,
Would never make a row like that,
E'en Majors on the martial field,
In point of lung to him must yield.

The heroes 'neath his high command,
An active, able, willing band,
Stand to their guns and inward quake
When his great shout the echoes wake.

And Houghton Fielden of the Straws,
Unused to "reign of terror" laws,
Flopped fairly down upon the floor,
When first he heard the awful roar.

While others quite mistake the sound
For shock of earthquake under ground,
And some in terror have been known
To swear the last Great Trump had blown.

'Mong Jackets on this flat I see,
A pugilistic devotee,
He rises from a warlike race
Descendant of the fighting Mace.

Down through departments still we go,
'Mid traders moving to and fro,
Through Mantles, Furs, and Jones's Cloths,
All guaranteed quite free from moths.

Here may be seen some lordly fellows,
And one I note among "Umbrellas,"
Who sports a flower and smells so grand,
He'd rival Rimmel's of the Strand.

But more of this I need not paint,
As I am not on satire bent,
So let us to the silks repair,
And look upon the worthies there.

Some figure gay in trowsers tight,
Of monster check and colour light,
With patent boots of narrow toe—
They're quite the present style you know;
N

Some wondrous cuts of whiskers too,
Here meet the keen observer's view;
One modest youth of pensive air,
Sports quite enough to stuff a chair.

And at the entrance from the "Yard,"
Pray who is he who stares so hard ?
With solemn visage long and queer,
Such as on Valentines appear.

The French department next we scan,
And 'mong the goods I see a man
Whose closely cropped and bristling hair
Suggests he's had a desperate scare.

For straight on end his wiry crop,
Looks upward like "Eternal Hope,"
Nor all the fine pomades in town
Can e'er avail to lay it down.

And one is here by best endeavour,
I urge of all to win his favour,
Who chance to sleep across the "Row,"
Sometimes he's locker-up you know.

And if you e'er get on the spree,
No hope is there at "number three,"
One minute late your doom is sure,
A night among the homeless poor.

Now through the Ribbons, Gloves, and Hose,
Go straight ahead, and 'fore your nose
You'll find the place of gaudy toys,
The pride of infant girls and boys.

There crying babes delight the ear,
And wooden men, and monkeys leer,
While peacocks strut and donkeys bray,
All in their most amusing way.

'Mong Ribbons, Gloves, and Hose and Laces,
I note indeed some wondrous faces,
But other parts attention need,
So we must hasten on with speed.

I cannot stop to mention all,
The short, the stout, the thin and tall
That swarm about all o'er the place,
Like bees at honey gathering pace;

But downwards still another stair,
Among De-laines and Costumes rare,
I hear the young men daily groan
Their sentiments by Telephone.

They've got that Yankee patent queer
Stretched from the Factory over here,
And when a message they convey
They ring the bell and bawl away.

But ere we seek the realms below
The mighty Counting House I'll show,
Where dandy clerks with ready quills
Are poring over books and bills.

Some sit high perched upon a stool—
Clerks like high places as a rule—
And some have sanctums glazed with care
To shield them from the vulgar stare.

Well drilled from youth to counting cash,
Some show at this great skill and dash;
But who can make the sovereigns twirl
So smart and neat as Mr Tyrrell?

I do not care to mention names,
Or else perhaps I'd speak of James,
Whose beaming face and merry eye
The cares of married life defy.

We reach the lower flat at length,
Where men and youths, in pride of strength,
Rush on in legions 'mid the gloom
Like dusky demons in each room.

Here on the left the "Dock" appears,
From whence loud voices reach our ears,
And one of extra vehement pitch
Belongs, I think, to Mr H——.

Down in that "Dock" for many a year
He's led a stormy, wild career,
And still it seems his greatest joy
To make a row with man and boy.

His leading Officer so bold
Is cast in Nature's largest mould,
And when along the Strand he steers
Folks think he's in the Grenadiers.

That fiercely twisted gay moustache
Gives him a pompous martial dash,
And as he walks each female sighs,
And casts on him admiring eyes.

We hail the "Town Room" now, and here
I beg to show you Charlie Beer,
Whom sporting critics justly call
A "tower of strength" when at football.

A portion labelled "A" to "G"
Contains a Gambling man I see;
But let us hope, despite his name,
He seldom tries the risky game.

And in the portion "H" to "P"
A comic sort of blade I see,

Who wears, they say, both day and night
That awful hat of colour light.

Here in the house or on the street
That ghostly hat you're sure to meet;
Where'er indeed you chance to go
It, phantom-like, moves to and fro.

But Fraser shines at "imitation,"
And meets with public approbation,
And makes an audience often screech
To hear his after dinner speech.

But now the room marked "R" to "Z"
Demands that notice should be paid
To one who shuns the female sex,
And wears a monstrous pair of "specs."

This gent of great importance hails
From pleasant land of ancient Wales,
Where brave Llewellyn's faithful hound
In song and story is renowned.

In "R" to "Z" he's monarch high,
And nought escapes his eagle eye;
His letter orders, come what may,
Must go per "Sutton" every day.

I do not wish your nerves to shock,
But round the corner from the "Dock"
(I vouch a fact apart from "chaff")
We have a living printo-graph.

The man to whom I give this name
Deserves his Caligraphic fame,
And ought to wear the legal wig,
Instead of overseeing "pig."

Now ere we leave the realms below,
The Commissariat Chief I'll show,
Great Gauntlett, whom we all revere,
He contracts for the food and beer.

He scans the butter and the cheese
To ascertain if mixed with grease,
And by-and-by, although he's loth,
Perhaps for supper he'll grant both.

But ere I bid my muse farewell,
We'll briefly glance at the Retail ;
One man is there of stature fine
Who well deserves a passing line.

When first his giant form you see
The question rises " Who is he? "
Ye gods! behold his whisker spears,
He seems the last of cavaliers.

In stylish garments fitting tight,
He towers erect a warehouse knight ;
E'en stately Guardsmen at Whitehall,
He proudly overtops them all.

And further round, a thoughtful face,
In which bright intellect I trace,
Proclaims a politician keen
In much respected Mr Green.

And last, but far from least, we say
Comes courteous, learned Mr Bray,
A useful member everywhere,
In business, council, and the chair.

A man whom bigotry ne'er knew,
So broad, so clear his every view ;
A leader in the social van—
A manly-hearted Englishman.

Now, as I close, I hope no heart
Feels rancour at my muses' dart,
For bad intention holds no sway
In aught that's said by JOHN S. RAE.

NOTE.—Although several of the points in this composition may not be quite intelligible to the general reader, yet the large number of London readers who have requested its insertion in this volume, gives it a claim to publication. Alas! the merry circle that hailed it first in recitation form in December 1881 at 72 St. Paul's Churchyard have not all been spared, though short the time, to hail it again in this volume. The hearty Scot that then did

> Figure gay in trousers tight,
> Of monster check and colour light,

now lies far from

> St Paul's Cathedral shade

in a green churchyard in Aberdeenshire, and he whose

> Closely cropped and bristling hair

is noticed in the piece, rests too in death in his native English soil, while many of those who are still in life

> Are severed far and wide
> By mount and stream and sea.

—◇—

The Black Watch.

(Left Edinburgh Castle for Egypt on 7th August, 1882.)

HURRAH! the gallant "Forty-Twa,"
The brave Black Watch, sae bold an' braw,
Wi' fearless tread they march awa'
Again frae Caledonia.

Edina's Castle-fortress rings,
As loud and wild the war-pipe sings
A daring song, whase music flings
Defiance oot to ony, O.

Let tyrants tremble at their tread,
And every despot bow his head,
Nor dare to tug the tartan plaid
That haps auld Caledonia.

Nor blazing suns, nor frost an' snaw
Can ever daunt the " Forty-Twa ; "
They crack the croons o' ane an' a'
    Their foes, tho' e'er sae mony, O.

By Scottish mountain, tarn an' glen
Were born an' bred those kilted men ;
An' weel they ken hoo to maintain
    The richts o' Caledonia.

In every clime their flag has waved,
An' mony a field of battle braved,
Where aye the " Forty-Twa " behaved
    Wi' skill an' courage bonnie, O.

Then glory to the " Forty-Twa,"
An' to oor gallant sodjers a',
For weel they've won the honours braw
    That deck auld Caledonia.

Endymion !

(Written on the appearance of the Earl of Beaconsfield's celebrated
Novel of that name.)

BEHOLD upon the world's stage
    The great sensation of the age ;
An oracle speaks from thy page,
    Endymion !

The greatest works must pale their fire,
    And to obscurity retire ;
All ask amazed, " Did gods inspire
    Endymion ? "

The midnight blasts, with hollow moan,
The magic name they waft it on,
And circling spheres in chorus groan
    Endymion !

Each wavelet of the rolling Thames
That used to murmur other names
Distinctly gurgles and acclaims
             Endymion!

Each cab that rattles o'er the Strand
Unites with every brazen band
To swell the awful echo grand—
             Endymion!

And when this old and dizzy world
Is from its mighty axis hurled,
A flag shall read, 'mid wrecks unfurled,
             Endymion!

—◇—

The Wedding.*

MUIRESK and Forglen join to-day
          In happy bonds of wedlock gay,
     And blythe the birds on every spray
     A merry song are singing :
     A merry song are singing,
     And the woodlands all are ringing,
     And the flags their folds are flinging
On the bosom of the day.

From Forglen's shady, sheltered bowers,
That nestle 'neath its stately towers,
The fairest of the lovely flowers
     Is woo'd across the Deveron :
     Is woo'd across the Deveron,
     Whose glassy waters quiverin'
     Run bright as they have ever run
Through summer's golden hours.

* The marriage of H. A. Farquhar Snottiswood, Esq. of Muiresk, to
Miss Abercromby of Forglen.

O, Deveron! wandering pilgrim old,
Whose cradle is the mountains bold,
Since first thy waters seaward roll'd,
  'Neath sun and moonbeam glancing :
  'Neath sun and moonbeam glancing,
  How many a tale entrancing,
  In ardent love's romancing,
Has by thy banks been told.

And many a blossom fair and gay,
That by thy banks first saw the day,
'S been woo'd and won and wed away
  Since time began his winging :
  Since time began his winging,
  And the forest choirs their singing ;
  But no sweeter music ringing
Ever rose than swells to-day.

Success attend the happy two,
May joys be rife and sorrows few,
And may their hearts be leal and true
  Together linked for ever :
  Together linked for ever
  In a wedlock none may sever,
  And the Star of Love, O! never
Be it clouded from their view.

Farewell to England's Daughter.

WHEN must thou go so soon, fair maid,
  While yet our greetings are but said,
While yet we homage scarce have paid,
  Or thou has seen old Scotia ?

Could'st thou not stay and hear the chime
Of Xmas bells in northern clime,
When "canny Scots" the cares of time
    Forget in blythe carousal?
Such pity 'tis to come and go,
And see us but 'mid winter's snow;
Thou must return when flowerets blow
    By woodland, stream, and mountain.
Then thou wilt grant old Scotia wild
Is Nature's first and fairest child,
And by her endless charms beguiled
    Thou'dst ever, ever tarry.
Oh! fair, indeed, are England's plains,
And rich her towns in commerce gains,
And there a subtle beauty reigns
    'Mong all her smiling daughters.
But to the land of Scott and Burns
The soul romantic ever turns,
A halo from the past adorns
    Each spot where'er we wander.
Then haste thee, haste thee back again,
And let our wish be not in vain,
That thou mayest soon with us remain
    To be no passing stranger.

Marriage Bells.*

MARRIAGE bells, for prince or peasant,
    Merrily they peal, and pleasant;
        Gaily ringing time is winging,
Lovers but of yesterday
Join in wedlock sweet to-day.
Thine be years of peaceful gladness,

* Written on the occasion of Prince Leopold's marriage, 27th April, 1882.

And the sombre shade of sadness,
  Haunting mortals, shun thy portals;
This the people wish for thee,
Leopold, Duke of Albany.
Bear thee proudly, ancient fame
Haloes o'er thy princely name ;
  Scottish mountains, Scottish fountains
Echo of thy title free,
Leopold, Duke of Albany.
In the heart with thine united
May the flame of love alighted
  Glow forever, waning never,
Till eternity's bright day
Mingle with its earthly ray.
In the gay and gilded palace
Pleasure high may hold her chalice,
  Brimming ever, empty never ;
But her sweetest draught is love,
Pure as dew from heaven above,
Falling free on Prince and vassal ;
Sacred boon in cot or castle ;
  Bosom cheering, home endearing
Thing of bright celestial birth,
Glowing sceptre of the earth.
Forged on seraph anvils ringing.
Shaped 'neath seraph hammers swinging,
  Magic moulded, it unfolded
All the genius of a plan
Formed to rule the fate of man.

—◇—

H.R.H. the Prince of Wales, K.G.

(On the occasion of His visit to Banff, Nov. 13th, 1883.)

HAIL ! Prince, all hail ! and as our welcomes ring
  We view in thee our noble, future King ;

Heir of the sceptre that a Bruce hath borne,
And all the honours that our Kings have worn.

Pure as the waters of our Scottish rills,
Old as our mountains and eternal hills,
Thy blood and name, O! Prince, illustrious heir
Of Britain's Crown, and her broad empire fair.

The land of tartans and the broad claymore,
That land hath welcomed thee, O! Prince, before ;
But ancient Banff hath summoned her array,
And doubly welcomes thee with pomp to-day.

Auld Scotia's heart is leal yet to the core,
And throbs as loyal as in days of yore ;
Her ruddy Lion on his field of gold
Yet glows unfettered with a visage bold.

Proud home of liberty, our hardy land
Ne'er felt the fetters of a conqueror's band ;
Greater than a Cæsar, thou on future day
Shalt reign where Cæsar never held the sway.

May health and happiness on thee attend,
To bless thy life unto a distant end,
Most noble Prince ; and may thy Princess see
And taste all pleasures that we wish to thee.

---♦---

Gladstone.

THY name, O! Gladstone, and thy fame so bright
    Shall live when ages shall have sunk in night;
    Great soul of liberty, may honoured bays
  Be thine, immortal to the latest days.
No Grecian hero of that iron time,
When war's red hand ruled every state and clime,

Shines half so brilliant from the page of Greece
As thou, great hero, from the page of peace.
A light supernal of the brightest ray,
Thy voice and gesture can the millions sway
In freedom's cause, and to their minds impart
That zeal for right which springeth in thy heart.
Thy noble teachings have no barren yield,
Nor fall they heedless on a rocky field ;
The social grain for harvest is nigh white,
When worth shall triumph over titled might.
Thou first of Statesmen of a mighty land,
With mind colossal as a leader grand,
Amid the peoples of a later age
A noble battle thou dost stoutly wage.
Thine eye, unerring in its eagle scan,
Can pierce time's mist, and see the goal of man
When generations of a race unborn
Shall look a tyrant in the face with scorn;
When lords must own the peasants of the land
As brothers formed by the self-same Hand,
And drain no longer from their slender store,
In sloth to revel as their sires of yore.
Then bliss shall sweeten labour's humble sphere,
And happiness shall wipe the bitter tear
So freely mingled with a life of toil,
And smiling plenty shall enrich the soil ;
And, learning more, still as the years roll on
The peoples hidden in oblivion
Shall end the work thou bravely hast begun,
And yield that homage thou hast truly won.

The Forglen Ball.*

'TIS whispered by the critics great,
   That 'mong the brilliant things of late,
      There shines resplendent o'er them all
The famous Mains of Forglen ball!

Sir Robert and his Lady fair,
To meet their tenantry were there;
And pouring in from every side,
They came—a joyous, happy tide.

The ladies, dress'd with care and taste,
Were genial all, and look'd their best;
And as for belles—they belles were all
That graced the famous Forglen Ball!

The music, too, was quite sublime—
Each measure had its proper time,
High o'er the dance, so light and free,
Loud swell'd the silv'ry melody.

The giddy waltz, in mazy ring,
With touches of the Highland fling,
Scottisches, polkas, reels, and all
Were danc'd at this eclipsing Ball!

And all the while the ladies smil'd
So sweet, an angel they'd beguil'd;
For had the angels human hearts,
They'd not be proof 'gainst Cupid's darts!

* The Forglen Ball was an entertainment given by Sir Robert Abercromby, Bart., to his tenantry, on the estates of Birkenbog, Forglen,
and Dunbuyas, on the occasion of his bringing home his " bonnie bride"
to his ancestral seat, Forglen House, situated on the banks of the
Devoron, near Turriff.

Ah! many a charming ankle there
Betray'd the owner's graces ràre,
And made the hearts of gallants bound
To love's sweet measure so profound;

And mark the gents, I pray you, too,
Who saunter with no aim in view;
But blandly smile on ladies all,
Or chat about the charming Ball!

While others deeper pleasure found
In handing fruits and wine around;
The ladies like a man, you know,
Who useful is for more than show.

Time ever seems to faster fleet
When youthful hearts with pleasure beat;
So did the pleasant hours but seem
The moments of some happy dream.

An hour or two, 'fore ope of day,
Dispersed this fam'd assembly gay;
Thus rave the critics, one and all,
About the famous Forglen Ball!

Forglen House.

'MID richly clustering vernal woods,
        O'erhanging Deveron's winding floods,
    Its stately turrets rise—
Home of our ancient Scottish race,
Renowned for valour and for grace,
    And deeds of enterprise.

See where yon monument is seen,
Uptowering through the forest's green,
    In memory of the brave

Of Abercromby's martial name,
Who fighting fell on fields of fame,
    And found a glorious grave.

When summer's sun falls on its towers,
And floods with gold the leafy bowers
    In all their vernal sheen,
And flashes on the standard old
That waves above its turrets bold,
    O! beauteous is the scene.

When Deveron, like a silvern band
That stretches through a fairy land,
    Rolls on its waters clear,
And sportsmen cast the luring fly,
O'er speckled beauties darting shy
    What artist's theme is here!

The stately homes of England old
Have oft been sung in measures bold
    By Saxon patriots true,
But our proud land of flood and fell
Of rugged rock and pleasant dell
    Hath homes of beauty too.

Where hardy Scotia's chieftians brave,
That led her sons on land and wave,
    Did first behold the light,
Bold men who guarded well the throne,
The people's interests and their own
    With iron hand of might;

Who counted aye the toiling one
A kinsman and a fellow-man
    That drew a kindred breath,
And stern together on the field,
As Scottish men their blades did wield
    Till victory or death.
o

And stately Forglen may'st thou stand
Long 'mid thy woods and waters grand,
   And hearts be nursed in thee—
That dearly lo'e auld Scotland's name,
Her people and her deathless fame—
   To all posterity.

The Lark.

HAIL! dusky minstrel of the wild,
   The star of morning's votive child,
     First herald of the sun;
On dew bespangled gladsome wing
Aloft thou soarest far to sing
     Ere day hath scarce begun.
Uprising from the yellow corn,
From out the mists of early morn,
     Clear rings thy matin song,
Triumphant over field and lea
High-swelling burst of minstrelsy,
     That wakes the feathered throng.
High o'er the clouds, up! up! away,
Thou tiny speck of sombre grey,
     The apex of thy goal
Is shrouded from our futile sight—
Where terminates thy raptured flight,
And sunburst of thy soul;
But like a string of pearls sweet,
Clear falling at our earth-bound feet,
     Thy mellow-throated strain
We hear, as if a silvern thread
'Twixt earth and thee far overhead
     Still bound thee unto men.
O! what is that within thy breast
That thrills and stirs thee from thy nest

To greet the opening day,
And bids thee sing on quivering wing
Till all the airy cloudlands ring—
    Resounding to thy lay?
Sweet sombre minstrel of the lea
Whence comes thy stream of melody
    Surpassing all the throng?
Rapt, matchless singer of the wild,
The star of morning's votive child
    Thou art the king of song.

—◇—

A Holiday Sketch.

ONE day in spring, when birds did sing,
    And Nature's face was sweet and fair,
A jovial three, from work set free,
    Resolved to sniff the country air.
We caught an early morning train
    That for the sunny south was bound,
On wings of steam through vales we sped,
    And darkling tunnels underground.
Past many a town of great renown
    In tales of ancient, warlike story,
And castles old where barons bold
    Upheld our Scottish name and glory.
By fair Edina, Scotia's pride,
    Still southward speeding quickly on,
We viewed her grand historic towers
    That in the morning sunlight shone.
And lo! as swift we pass them by,
    The sturdy lads of Gala water,
In peaceful mood, o'er many a rood,
    The golden grain in showers they scatter.
Those braes, where once the Southron ranged

In all the fierce array of battle,
Are covered now with browsing herds
Of sheep, and thriving Lowland cattle.
And now the stream of winding Tweed,
    O'erhung by "wildwoods thickening green,"
Rolls on its bright and classic tide,
    Like streak of silver through the scene.
See yonder antique hoary pile,
    As Melrose swift we're steaming by—
A sacred spot to Scotsmen dear,
    For there the Bruce's heart doth lie.
A monument of mighty sires,
    Reared in the ages of the past,
The grand old Abbey still doth stand,
    Through summer's sun and winter's blast.
Now Cowdenknowes salutes the eye,
    Robed in the varying blooms of spring,
Inspiring still the passing bard,
    In raptured notes its praise to sing.
E'en seen through mist and drizzling rain,
    A sombre beauty marks the scene ;
A spot with Nature's beauties decked—
    The garden of the Rustic Queen.
At Earlston we now arrive,
    And here awhile we mean to stay,
And taste the cheer the place affords
    E'er we resume our homeward way.
Conducted by our worthy friend,
    The host of Earlston Hotel—
A place that's famed the country round
    For good " Scot's drink" and pithy ale—
We soon are cosy by the fire,
    While creaks again the groaning board
Beneath the hospitable load
    That bounteous plenty there has stored.
A happy time we spent indeed,
    'Mong kindest friends in homely way,

And left resolved, like Death and Burns,
 To meet again some other day.
At Edinbro', as we homeward came,
 While changing trains 'neath cloud of night,
To gain new seats mid seething crowds
 Our desperate way we had to fight.
The mob o'er politics was mad,
 And Whig and Tory vehemence lent
To swell the ringing counter cheers
 In which they gave their feelings vent.
But home at last we safely reached,
 And sought the downy couch of rest,
Where balmy sleep our eyelids closed
 In dreamless slumber of the just.

—◇—

Maggie, Flower of Cornhill.

(To a young lady during her illness.)

VIRGIN snow-drop, lovely flower,
 May sweet health be soon thy dower,
 Decking, with its rosy glow,
 Once again thy cheek and brow.

All the flowers are now in bloom ;
Sunshine lights the world's gloom ;
Birds sing love in every tree,
Rise, and all would perfect be.

Maggie, flower of Cornhill,
Nature has one niche to fill
In its picture fair and free
With one blossom—that is thee.

Haste then, Maggie, leave thy bed,
And with lightsome, merry tread

Roam once more by wood and rill,
Bonnie flower of Cornhill.

E'er the summer blooms are gone,
Or the summer birds have flown,
Add thy presence to the scene,
Graceful, charming, fairy queen.

Virgin snow-drop, lovely flower,
May sweet health be soon thy dower,
Decking, with its rosy glow,
Once again thy cheek and brow.

Lines

On the Death of a very promising and beautiful young lady, who died
while on a visit at some distance from her home.

LIKE a rose, when the glory of summer has fled,
    That late in the beauty of bloom was arrayed,
    Lies Mary, our darling, beneath the green sod—
Her spirit has passed to the mansions of God.

She died from her home, but her mother was near
To 'tend the last bed of her darling so dear—
To whisper her comfort when passing away
To that land where no cloud ever shadows the day.

Fond parents may grieve o'er her that hath gone,
And left them lamenting, bereaved and alone,
But Mary is waiting 'mong angels of love,
To welcome them home to their Father above.

Oh! sweet is the thought that no partings are there,
When the world we leave, with its sorrows and care;
Ah! life's but a span, and we shortly shall hear
The song of the angels fall soft on the ear.

Then weep not for Mary, she blooms a bright flower,
The Hand that hath culled her can solace outpour,
As balm to the hearts of her sorrowing friends—
When He takes, He but takes to Himself what He
lends.

———◇———

Epistle to a Friend.

[I had received a book from my friend per post, and which, by some error,
was charged two or three shillings postage on delivery. On being
informed of this charge, by way of penance for the way in which the
book was sealed up, &c., he wrote a letter of lamentation to me on the
subject, which originated the ideas for the moralising epistle which I
here append.]

DEAR FRIEND, o'er trifles ne'er lament,
Nor count the money badly spent
That's spent in *Poesy's cause;
For still the Muse will make us spend
The cash as free as rhymes we've pen'd—
Such are her changeless laws.
No golden store she'll let us hord,
Such happiness (?) she'll not afford,
But such as springs from fame;
Her prompting voice still bids us look
Where on Parnassus fame's great book
Awaits our humble name;
For those to read who come behind,
And are in Poesy's mesh entwined
As fast, my friend, as we;
For, fight 'gainst fate howe'er they may,
They will be subject to her sway
Till death shall set them free.
'Tis better so, for wealth of gold
Could ne'er to me the sweets unfold
Of Poesy's raptured lore;

*The book referred to was a poetical MS. of sender's.

When she within my bosom reigns,
Pure bliss immingles with the strains
　　This heart of mine doth pour.
In that rapt hour such fancies rise,
And visions flit before my eyes,
　　As draw my soul from earth,
To revel in a brighter sphere,
And list to sounds with charmèd ear
　　That have no mortal birth.
Ah! give to me that magic hour
When glows my soul to feel the power
　　Which upward draws it on;
When lost to all around I gaze
With vacant glance thro' airy ways,
　　Wrapt in oblivion;
And in that hour what seraph voice
Is that which stirs me to rejoice,
　　And feel that 'yond this span,
When we have passed life's mortal gates,
A great eternity awaits
　　The deathless soul of man?
Is there a human wretch would own
Himself but monkey overgrown,
　　Who never felt that soul
Which heaven bestowed within him rise,
And tell him that he never dies,
　　Though countless ages roll?
If such there is, Great God inspire
Him with one spark of potent fire
　　To know the mystic way,
Where, led by Faith, men bravely tread,
In moral armour strong arrayed,
　　To purer, brighter day.

Letter to Mr James S.

ALL hail! again, my grey goose quill,
　　Thy point, besmeared with sable dews,
　　Can range obedient to my will
The flowery paths loved by the muse.
Hie then, my fancy, to the north,
　　And bring to view that friend of mine,
That man of talent and of worth—
　　Dear S--, my friend, of "Auld Lang Syne."
And, Jim, right glad was I to hear
　　Thy voice speak from the page again,
In accents still remembered dear
　　By me, thy brother of the pen.
I'm glad to think thou hast begun
　　To climb Parnassus' gilded steep,
Where Poesy's honours, nobly won,
　　Thy name and fame may safely keep.
Drink deep the Muse, soil not her wing
　　With flights immoral in their strain ;
But strike thy lyre, and nobly sing
　　To cheer the wretched heart again.
As for myself, I moralize thus :—
(What was the power that brought the hour
　　To bid my fancy stray,
And in the realms of Poesy wing
　　Its light and airy way ?
I may not reach the soaring peaks,
　　'Mong eagles there to plume,
Nor sink into the lowest deep
　　To sing unheard in gloom ;
But if my song should cheer one heart
　　That listens to its strain,
I cherish will the sweet belief
　　I have not sung in vain)--
Afar yet shines Fame's temple dome,
　　Wreathed in the mists of years to be,

With many a chequered path to roam
Before its portals we can see.
But gird thy loins, man for the fray,
And call to aid the "tuneful Nine,"
To guide thee o'er bright fancy's way,
Inspiring song and thought divine.
Far from the city's "madding strife,"
Far from the busy haunts of men,
Far from the wild vortex of life,
Far from the wretch's woe and pain,
You live at peace, and muse at will,
See Nature in each varying mood,
By heathy hill, and limpid rill,
By daisied lea, and waving wood;
While I, poor soul, mid smoke and gloom,
In this "queen city" of the west,
Am buried in a living tomb,
Unmarked, indeed, by hallowed rest.
Then dost thou really now intend
To bid adieu to Scotia's strand,
Across the wave thy way to bend
For fortune in a foreign land?
Where green the groves of myrtle spring,
And sweetest flowers perfume the air;
Where gaudy plumaged warblers sing
'Mong tropic blooms so rich and rare;
Or where the savage Zulu glides
So cunning on his fated prey;
With swift, unerring aim he guides
The deadly whizzing assegia.
Alluring Hope says mount my car,
And traverse climes and paths unknown,
A glorious harvest waves afar,
By wanderers only to be mown.
'Tis like the drum's inspiring voice
When gathering dark the legions wheel,
It stirs their spirits to rejoice,

And glory flashes from their steel.
Their standards to the winds are spread,
The breezes on their banners play ;
To conquest forth they're grandly led,
While hope to victory points the way.
I think there's field as good at home
For enterprise as far away ;
And patriot hearts should never roam
When inspiration bids them stay.
What's all the wealth and golden gain
That deep in Indian mines may lie ?
To soaring souls 'twould be a chain,
Beyond which they could never fly.
But now I think I've said enough,
The page of nonsense is quite full ;
I wait thy verdict on this stuff—
The teachings of the Muses' school.
Thy friend in need, thy friend indeed,
When here, or near, or far away,
Now ends this rhyming ranting screed,
And signs, yours ever, JOHN S. RAE.

To Mr A. H. P

Address of the employees of the Caledonian House, Glasgow, to Mr A. H.
P., on presenting him with a timepiece on the occasion of his marriage.

SIR, flattering speeches are ignoble things—
 The breath of puppets, and the bane of kings—
 But we to-night perform no courtier's part,
But speak the feelings of our inmost heart.

Thy fellow-workers of that house of fame,
Whose worthy labours have obtained its name,
To-night have gathered in thy presence here
To give this token of respect sincere.

To you, dear sir, esteemed alike by all—
From " heavies " downward to departments small—
This gift is tendered in their common name,
And bears inscription to attest the same.

Thy time of singleness has passed away,
And now the dawning of thy nuptial day
Breaks clear upon thee with its silvery light
To end for aye thy bacheloric night.

May peace and happiness thy steps attend,
And shed their charms around thee to the end;
And 'mid the sorrows and the joys of life,
May thy fair partner prove a loving wife.

Accept, then, sir, the tribute you deserve,
And, in the future, may its presence serve
To keep thee ever in the noble line,
And stir sweet memories of auld langsyne.

—◇—

To R. S. M.

FAIR sister of the tuneful throng,
　Companion of the Muses sweet,
　　Whose soul is eloquent with song,
　　As kindred spirit thee I greet,
　　And may thy strains with fervour beat
　　　For ever and for ever.

The hills eternal cannot stand,
　They sink and crumble to decay;
The restless sea outwears its strand,
　But Thought immortal lives for aye,
　And, living, passes not away
　　　For ever and for ever.

Fair sister of the tuneful throng,
  Upon Parnassus' sacred hill
You draw the spirit of thy song
  From out the Muses' mystic well—
A song whose melody shall swell
  For ever and for ever.

Companion of the Muses sweet,
  Fair sister of the tuneful throng,
As kindred spirit thee I greet,
  Whose soul is eloquent with song—
A friend of Right, a foe of Wrong
  For ever and for ever.

—◇—

Letter to Mr James Smith.

MY DEAR BROTHER BARD, I esteem and regard,
    I humbly admit I'm your debtor ;
  So I take my pen, for I really am fain
To answer your last welcome letter.
So your darling's away, oh, sad was the day
  She left you alone in your sorrow ;
But cheer up, my man, and be blythe as you can,
  And from Hope still some comfort you'll borrow.
I sincerely lament, and I often repent,
  That I asked not for her *carte-de-visite*,
As features so handsome are ever at ransom,
  And then 'twould be pleasant to quiz it.
See this week in the *Friend*, well nigh at the end,
  A fine song by that man* of the rail.
On pure Doric strings of his cronies he sings—
  'Tis a measure that never will fail.
But we too shall sing, while our fancy shall wing—
  Both the English and Scotch we can " do "—

* Anderson (Surfaceman).

And still shall we scribble, while Life's sands dribble,
   On all subjects both antique and new.
Here's health, minus wealth, to the men of the pen,
   For wealthy they never can be,
Since the Muse can but choose, and never refuse,
   Such cloud-skimming nobles as we.
The seekers for gold, in these times as of old,
   Have to search 'mong the dust and the clay ;
And the lower the digger the chance is the bigger
   Of bearing the nuggets away.
So heed not the cash, man, nor mentally lash, man,
   Yourself for the want o't, I pray ;
Enough is full plenty, so rest ye content aye,
   And strive for the laurel or bay.
When Sophie has crowned you with bliss, and around
      you
   The young olive branches may grow,
Just teach the young beauties of Life's stern duties,
   And how 'mid its dangers to row.
Then they'll think of the man and his wonderful
      plan
   Of existence so logic'ly clear,
Who seemed with his knowledge an animate college—
   A light 'mid the darkness so drear.
Now, I'll make as bold (as they say in rhymes old)
   To ask you to write me at once ;
Delay will sore grieve me, but friend do believe me,
   An answer your worth will enhance.
To this wish of "the bard" pay some small regard,
   Who toils here from home far away ;
He hardly needs mention, nor call your attention,
   To name, as per usual, JOHN RAE.

To a Couple of Young Ladies.

BEAUTEOUS, bright, angelic pair,
    Charming all you chance to meet;
Blooming in your beauty rare,
    Like two pretty rosebuds sweet.
As the stars of heaven that beam
    In the firmament above—
You, like centre planets, gleam
    In the firmament of love.

—◇—

Humorous Epitaphs.

I.

MAN was burned in F. E. G. (effigy),
    A place not learned by geography;
    When roast no crying e'er he made—
His boast was dying to his trade;
He dyed to live and lived to die,
No wonder he could fire defy.

II.

Below this heap of mossy mould
Repose a martyr's bones, I'm told;
He perished at the stake—in brief,
Was choked upon a steak of beef.

—◇—

Boldie's Epitaph.

HERE in a hole below this stane
    Puir Boldie's ashes lie;
    When Death took him I lost a frien'
On whom I could rely.

Alas! he only was a dog,
　Yet noble, brave, and true ;
An', reader, though you're not a dog,
　Can this be said of you?

———◇———

Gladstone's Epitaph.

WHEN states have sunk and thrones decayed,
　And lordly pomp have perished,
　　Thy name and fame that cannot fade
Shall be revered and cherished ;
For Right and Justice cannot die
While God's own throne is firm on high.

———◇———

Misfortune's vile an' bitter draught
　We aften hae to drink it,
An' 'cute's the man wha's head can plan
　A way to safely jink it ;
But drink it, or jink it, whichever best you can,
An' strive aye to thrive aye, an' be an honest man.